A CAMPFIRE GIRL'S FIRST COUNCIL FIRE

BY

JANE L. STEWART

The Camp Fire Girls

In the Woods

CHAPTER I

THE ESCAPE

"Now then, you, Bessie, quit your loafin' and get them dishes washed! An' then you can go out and chop me some wood for the kitchen fire!"

The voice was that of a slatternly woman of middle age, thin and complaining. She had come suddenly into the kitchen of the Hoover farmhouse and surprised Bessie King as the girl sat resting for a moment and reading.

Bessie jumped up alertly at the sound of the voice she knew so well, and started nervously toward the sink.

"Yes, ma'am," she said. "I was awful tired—an' I wanted to rest for a few minutes."

"Tired!" scolded the woman. "Land knows you ain't got nothin' to carry on so about! Ain't you got a good home? Don't we board you and give you a good bed to sleep in? Didn't Paw Hoover give you a nickel for yourself only last week?"

"Yes—an' you took it away from me soon's you found it out," Bessie flashed back. There were tears in her eyes, but she went at her dishes, and Mrs. Hoover, after a minute in which she glared at Bessie, turned and left the kitchen, muttering something about ingratitude as she went.

As she worked, Bessie wondered why it was that she must always do the work about the house when other girls were at school or free to play. But it had been that way for a long time, and she could think of no way of escaping to happier conditions. Mrs. Hoover was no relation to her at all. Bessie had a father and mother, but they had left her with Mrs. Hoover a long time before, and she could scarcely remember them, but she heard about them, her father especially, whenever she did something that Mrs. Hoover didn't like.

"Take after your paw—that's what you do, good-for-nothin' little hussy!" the farmer's wife would say. "Leavin' you here on our hands when he went away—an' promisin' to send board money for you. Did, too, for 'bout a year—an' since then never a cent! I've a mind to send you to the county farm, that I have!"

"Now, maw," Paw Hoover, a kindly, toil-hardened farmer, would say when he happened to overhear one of these outbursts, "Bessie's a good girl, an' I reckon she earns her keep, don't she, helpin' you like, round the place?"

"Earn her keep?" Mrs. Hoover would shrill. "She's so lazy she'd never do anythin' at all if I didn't stand over her. All she's good fer is to eat an' sleep—an' to hide off som'ere's so's she can read them trashy books when she ought to be reddin' up or doin' her chores!"

And Paw Hoover would sigh and retire, beaten in the argument. He knew his wife too well to argue with her. But he liked Bessie, and he did his best to comfort her when he had the chance, and thought there was no danger of starting a dispute with his wife.

Bessie finished her dishes, and then she went out obediently to the wood pile, and set to work to chop kindling. She had been up since daylight—and the sun rose early on those summer mornings. Every bone and muscle in her tired little body ached, but she knew well that Mrs. Hoover had been listening to the work of washing the dishes, and she dared not rest lest her taskmistress descend upon her again when the noise ceased.

Mrs. Hoover came out after she had been chopping wood for a few minutes and eyed her crossly.

"'Pears to me like you're mighty slow," she said, complainingly. "When you get that done there's butter to be made. So don't be all day about it."

But the wood was hard, and though Bessie worked diligently enough, her progress was slow. She was still at it when Mrs. Hoover, dressed in her black silk dress and with her best bonnet on her head, appeared again.

"I'm goin' to drive into town," she said. "An' if that butter ain't done when I get back, I'll—"

She didn't finish her threat in words, but Bessie had plenty of memories of former punishments. She made no answer, and Mrs. Hoover, still scowling, finally went off.

As if that had been a signal, another girl appeared suddenly from the back of the woodshed. She was as dark as Bessie was fair, a mischievous, black-eyed girl, who danced like a sprite as she approached Bessie. Her brown legs were bare, her dress was even more worn and far dingier than Bessie's, which was clean and neat. She was smiling as Bessie saw her.

"Oh, Zara, aren't you afraid to come here?" said Bessie, alarmed, although Zara was her best and almost her only friend. "You know what she said she'd do if she ever caught you around here again?"

"Yes, I know," said Zara, seating herself on a stump and swinging her legs to and fro, after she had kissed Bessie, still laughing. "I'm not afraid of her, though, Bessie. She'd never catch me—she can't run fast enough! And if she ever touched me—"

The smile vanished suddenly from Zara's olive skinned face. Her eyes gleamed.

"She'd better look out for herself!" she said. "She wouldn't do it again!"

"Oh, Zara, it's wrong to talk that way," said Bessie. "She's been good to me. She's looked after me all this time—and when I was sick she was ever so nice to me—"

"Pooh!" said Zara. "Oh, I know I'm not good and sweet like you, Bessie! The teacher says that's why the nice girls won't play with me. But it isn't. I know—and it's the same way with you. If we had lots of money and pretty clothes and things like the rest of them, they wouldn't care. Look at you! You're nicer than any of them, but they don't have any more to do with you than with me. It's because we're poor."

"I don't believe it's that, Zara. They know that I haven't got time to play with them, and that I can't ask them here, or go to their houses if they ask me. Some time—"

"You're too good, Bessie. You never get angry at all. You act as if you ought to be grateful to Maw Hoover for looking after you. Don't she make you work like a hired girl, and pay you nothin' for it? You work all the time—she'd have to pay a hired girl good wages for what you do, and treat her decently, beside. You're so nice that everyone picks on you, just 'cause they know they can do it and you won't hit back."

Glad of a chance to rest a little, Bessie had stopped her work to talk to Zara, and neither of the two girls heard a stealthy rustling among the leaves back of the woodshed, nor saw a grinning face that appeared around the corner. The first warning that they had that they were not alone came when a long arm reached out suddenly and a skinny, powerful hand grasped Zara's arm and dragged her from her perch.

"Caught ye this time, ain't I?" said the owner of the hand and arm, appearing from around the corner of the shed. "My, but Maw'll pickle yer when she gits hold of yer!"

"Jake Hoover!" exclaimed Bessie, indignantly. "You big sneak, you! Let her go this instant! Aren't you ashamed of yourself, hurtin' her like that?"

Zara, caught off her guard, had soon collected herself, and begun to struggle in his grasp like the wild thing she was. But Jake Hoover only laughed, leering at the two girls. He was a tall, lanky, overgrown boy of seventeen, and he was enjoying himself thoroughly. He seemed to have inherited all his mother's meanness of disposition and readiness to find fault and to take delight in the unhappiness of others. Now, as Zara struggled, he twisted her wrist to make her stop, and only laughed at her cries of pain.

"Let her go! She isn't hurting you!" begged Bessie. "Please, Jake, if you do, I'll help you do your chores to-night—I will, indeed!"

"You'll have to do 'em anyhow," said Jake, still holding poor Zara. "I've got a dreadful headache. I'm too sick to do any work to-night."

He made a face that he thought was comical. Zara, realizing that she was helpless against his greater strength, had stopped struggling, and he turned on her suddenly with a vicious glare.

"I know why you're hangin' 'round here," he said. "They took that worthless critter you call your paw off to jail jest now—and you're tryin' to steal chickens till he comes out."

"That ain't true!" she exclaimed. "My father never stole anything. They're just picking on him because he's a foreigner and can't talk as well as some of them—"

"They've locked him up, anyhow," said Jake. "An' now I'm goin' to lock you up, too, an' keep you here till maw comes home—right here in the woodshed, where you'll be safe!"

And despite her renewed struggling and Bessie's tearful protests, he kept his word, thrusting her into the woodshed and locking the great padlock on the door, while she screamed in futile rage, and kicked wildly at the door.

Then, with a parting sneer for Bessie, he went off, carrying the key with him.

"Listen, Zara," said Bessie, sobbing. "Can you hear me?"

"Yes. I'm all right, Bessie. Don't you cry! He didn't hurt me any."

"I'll try and get a key so I can let you out before she comes home. If she finds you in there, she'll give you a beating, just like she said. I've got to go churn some milk into butter now, but I'll be back as soon as ever I can. Don't you worry! I'll get you out of there all right."

"Please try, Bessie! I'm so worried about what he said about my father. It can't be true—but how would he ever think of such a story? I want to get home and find out."

"You keep quiet. I'll find some way to get you out," promised Bessie, loyally.

And, stirred to a greater anger than she had ever felt by Jake Hoover's bullying of poor Zara, she went off to attend to her churning.

Jake, as a matter of fact, was responsible for a good deal of Bessie's unhappiness. As a child he had been sickly, and he had continued, long after he had outgrown his weakness, and sprouted up into a lanky, raw-boned boy, to trade upon the fears his parents had once felt for him. Among boys of his own age he was unpopular. He had early become a bully, abusing smaller and weaker boys.

Bessie he had long made a mark for his sallies of wit. He taunted her interminably about the way her father and mother had left her; he pulled her hair, and practiced countless other little tricks that she could not resent. His father tried to reprove him at times, but his mother always rushed to his defence, and in her eyes he could do no wrong. She upheld him against anyone who had a bad word to say concerning him—and, of course, Bessie got undeserved rebukes for many of his misdeeds.

He soon learned that he could escape punishment by making it seem that she had done things of which he was accused, and, as his word was always taken against hers, no matter what the evidence was, he had only increased his mother's dislike for the orphaned girl.

The whole village shared Maw Hoover's dislike of Zara and her father. He had settled down two or three years before in an abandoned house, but no one seemed to understand how he lived. He disappeared for days at a time, but he seemed always to have money enough to pay his way, although never any more. And in the village there were dark rumors concerning him.

Gossip accused him of being a counterfeiter, who made bad money in the abandoned house he had taken for his own, and that seemed to be the favorite theory. And whenever chickens were missed, dark looks were cast at Zara and her father. He looked like a gypsy, and he would never answer questions about himself. That was enough to condemn him.

Bessie finished her churning quickly, and then went back, hoping either to make Jake relent or find some way of releasing the prisoner in the woodshed. But she could see no sign of Jake. The summer afternoon had become dark. In the west heavy black clouds were forming, and as Bessie looked about it grew darker and darker. Evidently a thunder shower was approaching. That meant that Maw Hoover would hurry home. If she was to help Zara she must make haste.

Jake, it seemed, had the only key that would open the padlock and Bessie, though she knew that she would be punished for it, determined to try to break the lock with a stone. She told Zara what she meant to do, and set to work. It was hard work, but her fingers were willing, and Zara's frightened pleading, as the thunder began to roar, and flashes of lightning came to her through the cracks in the woodshed, urged her on. And then, just as she was on the verge of success, she heard Jake's coarse laugh in her ear. "Look out!" he shouted.

He stood in the kitchen door, and, as she turned, something fell, hissing, at her feet. She started back, terrified. Jake laughed, and threw another burning stick at her. He had taken a shovelful of embers from the fire, and now he tossed them at her so that she had to dance about to escape the sparks. It was a dangerous game, but one that Jake loved to play. He knew that Bessie was afraid of fire, and he had often teased her in that fashion. But suddenly Bessie shrieked in real terror. As yet, though the approaching storm blackened the sky, there was no rain. But the wind was blowing almost a gale, and Bessie saw a little streamer of flame run up the side of the woodshed.

"The shed's on fire! You've set it on fire!" she shrieked. "Quick—give me that key!"

Jake, really frightened then, ran toward her with the key in his hand.

"Get some water!" Bessie called to him. "Quick!"

And she unlocked the padlock and let Zara, terrified by the fire, out. But Jake stood there stupidly, and, fanned by the wind, the flames spread rapidly.

"Gosh, now you have done it!" he said. "Maw'll just about skin you alive for that when I tell her you set the shed afire!"

Bessie turned a white face toward him.

"You wouldn't say that!" she exclaimed.

But she saw in his scared face that he would tell any lie that would save him from the consequences of his recklessness. And with a sob of fright she turned to Zara.

"Come, Zara!" she cried. "Get away!"

"Come with me!" said Zara. "She'll believe you did it! Come with me!"

And Bessie, too frightened and tired to think much, suddenly yielded to her fright, and ran with Zara out into the woods.

CHAPTER II

AN UNJUST ACCUSATION

They had not gone far when the rain burst upon them. They stuck to the woods to avoid meeting Maw Hoover on her way home, and as the first big drops pattered down among the trees Zara called a halt.

"It's going to rain mighty hard," she said. "We'd better wait here and give it a chance to stop a little before we cross the clearing. We'll get awful wet if we go on now."

Bessie, shivering with fright, and half minded, even now, to turn back and take any punishment Maw Hoover chose to give her, looked up through the trees. The lightning was flashing. She turned back—and the glare of the burning woodshed helped her to make up her mind to stay with Zara. As they looked the fire, against the black background of the storm, was terrifying in the extreme.

"You'd never think that shed would make such a blaze, would you?" said Zara, trembling. "I'd like to kill that Jake Hoover! How did he set it on fire?"

"He must have been watching me all the time when I was trying to help you to get out," said Bessie. "Then, when I was nearly done, he called to me, and then he began throwing the burning wood at me. He knows I hate that—he's done it before. I can always get out of the way. He doesn't throw them very near me, really. But two or three times the sparks have burned holes in my dress and Maw Hoover's been as mad as she could be. So she thinks anyhow that I play around the fire, and she'd never believe I didn't do it."

"The rain ought to put the fire out," said Zara presently, after they had remained in silence for a few moments. "But I think it's beginning to stop a little now."

"It is, and the fire's still burning, Zara. It seems to me it's brighter than ever. And listen—when it isn't thundering. Don't you hear a noise as if someone was shouting back there?"

Zara listened intently.

"Yes," she said. "And it sounds as if they were chopping with axes, too. I hope the fire hasn't spread and reached the house, Bessie."

Bessie shivered.

"I hope so, too, Zara. But it's not my fault, anyhow. You and I know that, even if no one believes us. It was Jake Hoover who did it, and he'll be punished for it some time, I guess, whether his maw ever finds it out or not."

They waited a few minutes longer for the rain to stop, and then, as it grew lighter, they began to move on. They could see a heavy cloud of smoke from the direction of the farmhouse, but no more flames, and now, as the thunder grew more and more distant, they could hear shouting more plainly. Evidently help had come—Paw Hoover, probably, seeing the fire, and rushing up from the fields with his hired men and the neighbors to put it out.

"Zara," said Bessie, suddenly, "suppose Jake was telling the truth? Suppose they have taken your father away? You know they have said things about him, and lots of people believe he is a bad man. I never did. But suppose they really have taken him, what will you do?"

"I don't know. Stay there, I suppose. But, Bessie, it can't be true!"

"Maybe they wouldn't let you stay. When Mary Morton's mother died last year and left her alone, they took her to the poorhouse. Maybe they'd make you go there, too."

"They shan't!" cried Zara, her eyes flashing through her tears. "I—I'll run away—I'll do anything—"

"I'm going to run away, myself," said Bessie, quietly. She had been doing a lot of thinking. "No one could make me work harder than Maw Hoover, and they'd pay me for doing it. I'm going to get as far away as I can and get a real job."

Zara looked at Bessie, usually so quiet and meek, in surprise. There was a determined note in Bessie's voice that she had never heard there before.

"We'll stick together, you and I, Zara," said Bessie. "I'm afraid something has happened to your father. And if that's so, we'd better not go right up to your house. We'd better wait until it's dark, and go there quietly, so that we can listen, and see if there's anyone around looking for you."

"But we won't get any supper!" said poor Zara. "And I'm hungry already!"

"We'll find berries and nuts, and we can easily find a spring where we can drink all we want," said Bessie. "I guess we've got to look out for ourselves now, Zara. There's no one else to do it for us."

And Bessie, the meek, the quiet, the subdued, from that moment took command. Always before Zara had seemed the plucky one of the two. She had often urged Bessie to rebel against Maw Hoover's harshness, and it had been always Bessie who had hung back and refused to do anything that might make trouble. But now, when the time for real action had come, and Bessie recognized it, it was she who made the plans and decided what was to be done.

Bessie knew the woods well, far better than Zara. Unerringly she led the way to a spot she knew, where a farm had been allowed to drift back to wild country, and pointed out some cherry trees.

"Some berries aren't good to eat, but I know those cherries," said Bessie. "They used to be the best trees in the whole county years ago—Paw Hoover's told me that. Some believe that they're no good now, because no one has looked after the trees, but I know they're fine. I ate some only the other day, and they're ripe and delicious. So we'll have supper off these trees."

Zara, as active as a little cat, climbed the tree at once, and in a moment she was throwing down the luscious fruit to Bessie, who gathered it in her apron and called to Zara when she had picked enough of the big, round cherries.

"Aren't they good, Zara? Eat as many as you want. They're not like a real supper of meat and potatoes and things like that, you know, but they'll keep us from feeling hungry."

"They certainly will, Bessie. I'd never have known about them. But then I haven't lived long enough in the country to know it the way you do. I've been in cities all my life."

"Yes, and if we get to the city, Zara, you'll know lots of things and be able to tell me all about them. It must be wonderful."

"I suppose it is, Bessie, but I never thought of it that way. It must have been because I was used to everything of that sort. When you see things every day you get so that you don't think anything about them. I used to laugh at people from the country when I'd see them staring up at the high buildings, and jumping when an automobile horn tooted anywhere near them."

"I suppose it must have seemed funny to you."

"Yes, but I was sorry when I came out here and saw that everyone was laughing at me. There were all sorts of things I'd never seen or thought about. I'm really only just beginning to get used to them now. Bessie, it's getting pretty dark. Won't the moon be up soon?"

"Not for an hour or two yet, Zara. But it is dark now—we'd better begin walking toward your house. We want to get there while it stays dark, and before the old moon does get up. It'll be just as bright as daylight then, and they'd be able to see us. I tell you what—we want to keep off the road. We'll go through the woods till we get a chance to cut through Farmer Weeks' cornfield. That'll bring us out behind your place, and we can steal up quietly."

"You'd think we'd been doing something wrong, Bessie. It seems mighty mean for us to have to sneak around that way."

"It's all right as long as we know we haven't done anything that isn't right, Zara. That's the chief thing. If you do right, people will find it out sooner or later, even if they think at first that you're bad. Sometimes it takes a long time, but Paw Hoover says he's never known it to fail that a bad man gets found out sooner or later."

"Then Jake Hoover'd better look out," said Zara, viciously. "He's lied so much, and done so many mean things that you've got the blame for, that he'll have an awful lot to make up for when he starts in. What would Paw Hoover do to him if he knew he'd set the woodshed on fire, Bessie?"

"I don't know. He'd be awful mad. He hasn't got so awful much money, you know, and he needs it all for the farm. But Maw Hoover thinks Jake's all right. She'd find some excuse for him. She always does when he does get found out. That happens sometimes, you know. He can't always make them think I've done it."

"I guess maybe that's why he's so mean, Bessie. Don't you think so?"

"Shouldn't wonder, Zara. I don't believe he stops to think half the time. Here we are! We'll cut through the fence. Careful as we go through—keep to the lanes between the stalks. We mustn't hurt the corn, you know."

"I'd like to pull up every stalk! These people 'round here have been mean and ugly to my father ever since we came here."

"That isn't right, though, Zara. It won't do you any good to hurt them in return. If you do wrong, too, just because they have, you'll be just as bad as they are."

"Oh, I know, but they've said all sorts of awful things, and if they've put him in prison now—" She stopped, with a sob, and Bessie took her hand.

"Cheer up, Zara. We don't know that anything of that sort has happened yet, and, even if it has, it will come out all right. If your father hasn't done anything wrong, they can't punish him. He'll get a fair trial if he's been arrested, and they can't prove he's done anything unless he has, you know."

"But if they lied about him around here, mightn't they lie the same afterward—at the trial, Bessie? I'm frightened; really I am!"

"Hush, Zara! There's your house, and there's a light! That means there's someone there. I hope it's your father, but it might be someone else, and we mustn't let them hear us."

The two girls were out of the cornfield now, and, crossing a little patch of swampy land, came to the little garden around Zara's house, where her father had planted a few vegetables that helped to feed him and Zara.

The house was little better than a cabin, a rough affair, tumbled down in spots, with a sagging roof, and stained and weather-worn boards. It had no second floor at all, and it was a poor, cheap apology for a dwelling, all around. But, after all, it was Zara's home, the only home she knew, and she was so tired and discouraged that all she wanted was to get safely inside and throw herself down on her hard bed to sleep.

"Listen!" whispered Bessie, suddenly.

From the room into which the kitchen led there came a murmur of voices. At first, though they strained their ears, they could make nothing out of the confused sounds of talk. But gradually they recognized voices, and Bessie turned pale as she heard Paw Hoover's, easy for her to know, since his deep tones rumbled out in the quiet night. Zara recognized them, too, and clutched Bessie's arm.

"My father isn't there!" she whispered. "If he was, I'd hear him."

"There's Farmer Weeks—and I believe that's Jake Hoover's voice, too," said Bessie, also in a whisper.

Then the door was opened, and the two girls huddled closer together, shivering, afraid that they would be discovered. But it seemed that Paw Hoover had only opened the door to get a little air, since the night was very hot after the storm. About them the insects were making their accustomed din, and a little breeze rustled among the treetops. But, with the door open, they could hear what was being said plainly enough.

"I ain't goin' to wait here all night, Brother Weeks," said Paw Hoover. "Got troubles enough of my own, what with the woodshed settin' fire to the house!"

"Oh!" whispered Bessie. "Did you hear that, Zara? It was worse than we thought."

"Huh!" said Weeks, a rough, hard man, who found it hard to get men to work when he needed them for the harvest every summer, on account of his reputation for treating his men badly.

"I allus told you you'd have trouble with that baggage afore you got rid of her, Paw! Lucky that she didn't burn you out when you was all asleep—I say," said Jake.

Bessie listened, every nerve and muscle in her body tense. They blamed her for the fire, then! Her instinct when she had run away had been right.

"I swan, I dunno what all possessed her," said Paw Hoover. "We give her a good home—but Jake here seen her do it, though he was too late to stop her—hey, Jake?"

"That's right, Pop," said Jake. "She didn't know I was aroun' anywhere. Say, you ought to have her pinched for doin' it, too."

"I dunno—she's only a youngster," said Paw. "I guess they wouldn't hold her responsible, somehow. But say, Brother Weeks, I hate to think of that little

Zara runnin' roun' the woods to-night. She ain't done nothin' wrong, even if her paw's a crook. An' now they took him off, who's a-goin' to look out for her?"

"I'll drive her over to the poor-farm when she turns up," said Weeks. "Then they'll take her, an' apprentice her to someone as wants a girl to work aroun' his place, like. Bind her over till she's twenty-one, and let her work for her keep. I might take her myself—guess 'twouldn't cost such a lot to feed her. She's thin—reckon she ain't ever had much to eat here."

Bessie, feeling the tremor in Zara's rigid body at this confirmation of her worst fears, put her hand quickly over her friend's mouth, just in time to check a cry that was rising to her lips.

"Come, Zara," she whispered, gently. "We'll have to look out for ourselves. Come, we'll get away. We mustn't stay around here."

And, holding Zara's arm, she led her away. For a long time, until Bessie judged that it was safe to return to the road, they kept on through the woods. And, when they came out on the road, the moon was up.

"The world's a beautiful place after all, Zara," said Bessie. "It can't be so bad when everything's so lovely. Come on, we'll walk a little further, and then we'll come to a place I know where we can sleep to-night—a place where wood cutters used to stay. No one's there now, and we'll be dry and safe."

"I'm not afraid if I'm with you, Bessie," said Zara.

CHAPTER III

WO-HE-LO

Two or three miles further along the road, Bessie spied the landmark she had been looking for.

"We'll turn off here," she said, "Cheer up, Zara. It won't be long now before we can go to sleep."

The full moon made it easy to pick their way along the wood path that Bessie followed, and before long they came to a small lake. On its far side, among the trees near the shore, a fire was burning, flickering up from time to time, and sending dancing shadows on the beach.

"There's someone over there, Bessie," said Zara, frightened at the sign of human habitation.

"They won't hurt us, Zara," said Bessie, stoutly. "Probably they won't even know that we're around, if we don't make any noise, or any fire of our own. Here we are—here's the hut! See? Isn't it nice and comfortable? Hurry now and help me to pick up some of these branches of pine trees. They'll make a comfortable bed for us, and well sleep just as well as if we were at home—or a lot better, because there'll be no one to be cross and make trouble for us in the morning."

Bessie arranged the branches, and in a few moments they were asleep, lying close together. Pine branches make an ideal bed, but, even had their couch been uncomfortable, the two girls would have slept well that night; they were too tired to do anything else. It was long after midnight, and both had been through enough to exhaust them. The sense of peace and safety that they found in this refuge in the woods more than made up for the strangeness of their surroundings, and when they awoke the sun was high. It was the sound of singing in the sweet, fresh voices of girls that aroused them in the end. And Bessie, the first to wake up, aroused Zara, and then peeped from the door of the cabin.

There on the beach, their hair spread out in the sun, were half a dozen girls in bathing dresses. Beside them were a couple of canoes, drawn up on the beach, and they were laughing and singing merrily as they dried their hair. Looking over across the lake, in the direction of the fire she had seen the night before, Bessie saw that it was still burning. A pillar of smoke rose straight in the still air, and beyond it, gleaming among the trees, Bessie saw the white sides of three or four tents. Astonished, she called Zara.

"They're not from around here, Zara," she whispered, not ready yet for the strangers to discover her. "Girls around here don't swim—it's only the boys who do that."

"I'll bet they're from the city and here on a vacation," said Zara.

"They look awful happy, Zara. Isn't that lady with the brown hair pretty? And she's older than the rest, too. You can see that, can't you?"

"Listen, Bessie! She just called one of the girls. And did you hear what she called her? Minnehaha—that's a funny name, isn't it?"

"It's an Indian name, Zara. It means Laughing Water. That's the name of the girl that Hiawatha loved, in the poem. I've read that, haven't you?"

"I've never been able to read very much, Bessie. But that girl isn't an Indian. She's ever so much lighter than I am—she's as fair as you. And Indians are red, aren't they?"

"She's not an Indian, Zara. That's right enough. It must be some sort of a game. Oh, listen!"

For the older girl, the one Zara had pointed out, had spied Bessie's peeping face suddenly.

"Look, girls!" she cried, pointing.

And then, without a word of signal all the girls suddenly broke out into a song—a song Bessie had never heard before.

"Wohelo for aye, Wohelo for aye,

Wohelo, Wohelo, Wohelo for aye;

Wohelo for work, Wohelo for health,

Wohelo, Wohelo, Wohelo for love!"

As they ended the song, all the girls, with laughing faces, followed the eyes of their leader and looked at Bessie, who, frightened at first when she saw that she had been discovered, now returned the look shyly. There was something so kind, so friendly, about the manner of these strange girls that her fear had vanished.

"Won't you come out and talk to us?" asked the leader of the crowd.

She came forward alone toward the door of the cabin, looking at Bessie with interest.

"My name is Wanaka—that is, my Camp Fire name," said the stranger. "We are Manasquan Camp Fire Girls, you know, and we've been camping out by this lake. Do you live here?"

"No—not exactly, ma'am," said Bessie, still a little shy.

"Then you must be camping out, too? It's fun, isn't it? But you're not alone, are you? Didn't I see another head peeping out?"

"That's Zara. She's my friend, and she's with me," said Bessie. "And my name's Bessie King."

She looked curiously at Wanaka. Bessie had never heard of the Camp Fire Girls, and the great movement they had begun, meant to do for American girls what the Boy Scout movement had begun so well for their brothers.

"Well, won't you and Zara spend the day with us, if you are by yourselves?" asked Wanaka. "We'll take you over to camp in the canoes, and you can have dinner with us. We're going back now to cook it. The other girls have begun to prepare it already."

"Oh, we'd like to!" cried Bessie. "I'm awfully hungry—and I'm sure Zara is, too."

Bessie hadn't meant to say that. But the thought of a real meal had been too much for her.

"Hungry!" cried Wanaka. "Why, haven't you had breakfast? Did you oversleep?"

She looked about curiously. And Bessie saw that she could not deceive this tall, slim girl, with the wise eyes that seemed to see everything.

"We—we haven't anything to eat," she said. And suddenly she was overcome with the thought of how hard things were going to be, especially for Zara, and tears filled her eyes.

"You shall tell me all about it afterwards," said Wanaka, with decision. "Just now you've got to come over with us and have something to eat, right away. Girls, launch the canoes! We have two guests here who haven't had any breakfast, and they're simply starving to death."

Any girls Bessie had ever known would have rushed toward her at once, overwhelming her with questions, fussing around, and getting nothing done. But these girls were different. They didn't talk; they did things. In a moment, as it seemed, the canoes were in the water, and Bessie and Zara had been taken into different boats. Then, at a word from Wanaka, the paddles rose and dipped into the water, and with two girls paddling each canoe, one at the stern and one at the bow, they were soon speeding across the lake, which, at this point, was not more than a quarter of a mile wide.

Once ashore, Wanaka said a few words to other girls who were busy about the fire, and in less than a minute the savory odor of frying bacon and steaming coffee rose from the fire. Zara gave a little sigh of perfect content.

"Oh, doesn't that smell good?" she said.

Bessie smiled.

"It certainly does, and it's going to taste even better than it smells," she answered, happily.

They sat down, cross-legged, near the fire, and the girls of the camp, quiet and competent, and asking them no questions, waited on them. Bessie and Zara weren't used to that. They had always had to wait on others, and do things for other people; no one had ever done much for them. It was a new experience, and a delightful one. But Bessie, seeing Wanaka's quiet eyes fixed upon her, realized that the time for explanations would come when their meal was over.

And, sure enough, after Bessie and Zara had eaten until they could eat no more, Wanaka came to her, gently, and took her by the hand. She seemed to recognize that Bessie must speak for Zara as well as for herself.

"Now suppose we go off by ourselves and have a little talk, Bessie," she suggested. "I'm sure you have something to tell me, haven't you?"

"Yea, indeed, Miss Wanaka," said Bessie. She knew that in Wanaka she had found, by a lucky chance, a friend she could trust and one who could give her good advice.

Wanaka smiled at her as she led the way to the largest of the tents.

"Just call me Wanaka, not Miss Wanaka," she said. "My name is Eleanor Mercer, but here in the camp and wherever the Camp Fire Girls meet we often call one another by our ceremonial names. Some of us—most of us—like the old Indian names, and take them, but not always."

"Now," she said, when they were alone together in the tent, "tell me all about it, Bessie. Haven't you any parents? Or did they let you go out to spend the night all alone in the woods that way?"

Then Bessie told her the whole story. Wanaka watched her closely as Bessie told of her life with the Hoovers, of her hard work and drudgery, and of Jake's persecution. Her eyes narrowed slightly as Bessie described the scene at the woodshed, and told of how Jake had locked Zara in to wait for her mother's return, and of his cruel and dangerous trick with the burning embers.

"Did he really tell his father that you had set the shed on fire—and on purpose?" asked Wanaka, rather sternly.

"He was afraid of what would happen to him if they knew he'd done it," said Bessie. "I guess he didn't stop to think about what they'd do to me. He was just frightened, and wanted to save himself."

Wanaka looked at her very kindly.

"These people aren't related to you at all, are they?" she asked. "You weren't bound to them—they didn't agree to keep you any length of time and have you work for them in return for your board?"

"No," said Bessie.

"Then, if that's so, you had a right to leave them whenever you liked," said Wanaka, thoughtfully. "And tell me about Zara. Who is her father? What does he do for a living?"

"I don't believe she even knows that herself. They used to live in the city, but they came out here two or three years ago, and he's never gone around with the other men, because he can't speak English very well. He's some sort of a foreigner, you see. And when they took him off to prison Zara was left all alone. He used to stay around the cabin all the time, and Zara says he would work late at night and most of the day, too, making things she never saw. Then he'd go off for two or three days at a time, and Zara thought he went to the city, because when he came back he always had money—not very much, but enough to buy food and clothes for them. And she said he always seemed to be disappointed and unhappy when he came back."

"And the people in the village thought he was a counterfeiter—that he made bad money?"

"That's what Maw Hoover and Jake said. They thought so, I know."

"People think they know a lot when they're only guessing, sometimes, Bessie. A man has a right to keep his business to himself if he wants to, as long as he doesn't do anything that's wrong. But why didn't Zara stay? If her father was cleared and came back, they couldn't keep her at the poor-farm or make her go to work for this Farmer Weeks you speak of."

"I don't know. She was afraid, and so was I. They call her a gypsy because she's so dark. And people say she steals chickens. I know she doesn't, because once or twice when they said she'd done that, she'd been in the woods with me, walking about. And another time I saw a hawk swoop down and take one of Maw Hoover's hens, and she was always sure that Zara'd done that."

Wanaka had watched Bessie very closely while she told her story. Bessie's clear, frank eyes that never fell, no matter how Wanaka stared into them, seemed to the older girl a sure sign that Bessie was telling the truth.

"It sounds as if you'd had a pretty hard time, and as if you hadn't had much chance," she said, gravely. "It's strange about your parents."

Bessie's eyes filled with tears.

"Oh, something must have happened to them—something dreadful," she said. "Or else I'm sure they would never have left me that way. And I don't believe what Maw Hoover was always saying—that they were glad to get rid of me, and didn't care anything about me."

"Neither do I," said Wanaka. "Bessie, I want to help you and Zara. And I think I can—that we all can, we Camp Fire Girls. You know that's what we live for—to help people, and to love them and serve them. You heard us singing the Wohelo cheer when we first saw you. Wohelo means work, and health, and love. You see, it's a word we made up by taking the first two letters of each of those words. I tell you what I'm going to do. You and Zara must stay with us here to-day. The girls will look after you. And I'm going into the village and while I'm there I'll see how things are."

"You won't tell Maw Hoover where we are; or Farmer Weeks?" cried Bessie.

"I'll do the right thing, Bessie," said Wanaka, smiling. "You may be sure of that. I believe what you've told me—I believe every word of it. But you'd rather have me find out from others, too, I'm sure. You see, it would be very wrong for us to help girls to run away from home. But neither you nor Zara have done that, if your story is right. And I think it is our duty to help you both, just as it is our pleasure."

CHAPTER IV

AN UNEXPECTED FRIEND

Bessie wasn't afraid of what Wanaka would find out in Hedgeville. Wanaka wouldn't take Jake Hoover's word against hers, that much was sure. And she guessed that Wanaka would have her own ways of discovering the truth. So, as Wanaka changed from her bathing suit to a costume better suited to the trip to the village, Bessie went out with a light heart to find Zara. Already she thought that she saw the way clear before them. With friends, there was no reason why they should not reach the city and make their own way there, as plenty of other girls had done. And it seemed to Bessie that Wanaka meant to be a good friend.

"Oh, Bessie, have you been hearing all about the Camp Fire, too?" asked Zara, when she espied her friend, "It's wonderful! They do all sorts of things. And Minnehaha is going to teach me to swim this afternoon. She'll teach you, too, if you like."

But Bessie only smiled in answer. She could swim already, but she said nothing about it, since no one asked her, seeming to take it for granted that, like Zara, she was unused to the water. Moreover, while she could swim well enough, she was afraid that she would look clumsy and awkward in comparison to the Camp Fire Girls. Most of them had changed their clothes now, before dinner.

Some wore short skirts and white blouses; one or two were in a costume that Bessie recognized at once as that of Indian maidens, from the pictures she had seen in the books she had managed to get at the Hoover farmhouse. She noticed, too, that many of them now wore strings of beads, and that all wore rings. Two or three of the girls, too, wore bracelets, strangely marked, and all had curious badges on their right sleeves.

"We've got to wash the dishes, now," said Minnehaha, who bore out her name by laughing and smiling most of the time. She had already told Zara that her real name was Margery Burton. "You sit down and rest, and when we've done, we'll talk to you and tell you more about the Camp Fire Girls and all the things we do."

"No, indeed," said Bessie, laughing back. "That won't do at all. You cooked our meal; now we'll certainly help to clean up. That's something I can do, and I'm going to help."

Zara, too, insisted on doing her share, and the time passed quickly as the girls worked. Then, when the things were cleaned and put away, and some preparations had been made for the evening meal, Zara begged to have her first swimming lesson at once.

"No, we'll have to wait a little while for that," said Minnehaha. "We must wait until Wanaka comes back. She's our Guardian, you see, and it's a rule that we mustn't go into the water unless she's here, no matter how well we swim, unless, of course, we have to, to help someone who is drowning. And it's too soon after dinner, too. It's bad for you to go into the water less than two hours after a meal. We're always careful about that, because we have to be healthy. That's one of the chief reasons we have the Camp Fire."

"Tell us about it," begged Zara, sitting down.

"You see this ring?" said Minnehaha, proudly.

She pointed to her ring, a silver band with an emblem,—seven fagots.

"We get a ring like that when we join," she explained. "That's the Wood-Gatherer's ring, and the National Council gives it to us. Those seven fagots each stand for one of the seven points of the law of the fire."

"What are they, Minnehaha?"

"They're easy to remember: 'Seek Beauty; Give Service; Pursue Knowledge; Be Trustworthy; Hold on to Health; Glorify Work; Be Happy.' If you want to do all those things—and I guess everyone does—you can be a Wood-Gatherer. Then, later on, you get to be a Fire-Maker, and, after that, a Torch-Bearer. And when you get older, if you do well, you can be a Guardian, and be in charge of a Camp Fire yourself. You see, there are Camp Fires all over. There are a lot of them in our city, and in every city. And there are more and more all the time. The movement hasn't been going on very long, but it's getting stronger all the time."

"Are you a Fire-Maker?"

"Not yet. If I were, I'd wear a bracelet, like Ayu. And instead of just having a bunch of fagots on my sleeve, there'd be a flame coming from them. And then, when I get to be a Torch-Bearer, I'll have a pin, as well as the ring and the bracelet, and there'll be smoke on my badge, as well as fire and wood. But you have to work hard before you can stop being a Wood-Gatherer and get to the higher ranks. We all have to work all the time, you see."

"I've had to work, too," said Bessie. "But this seems different because you enjoy your work."

"That's because we like to work. We work because we want to do it, not because someone makes us."

"Yes, I was thinking of that. I always worked because I had to—Maw Hoover made me."

"Who's Maw Hoover, Bessie?"

So Bessie told her story, or most of it, all over again, and the other girls, seeing that she was telling a story, crowded around and listened.

"I think it's a shame you were treated so badly," said Minnehaha. "But don't you worry—Miss Eleanor will know what to do. She won't let them treat you unfairly. Is she going to find out about things in the village?"

"Yes."

"Well, you needn't worry any more, then. Why, one of the first things she did in the city, when she started this Camp Fire, was to get us all to work to get better milk for the babies in the poor parts, where the tenement houses are. We all helped, but she did most of it. And now all the milk is good and pure, and the babies don't die any more in the hot weather in summer."

"That's fine. I'd like to be a Camp Fire Girl."

"Why shouldn't you be one, then?"

"But—"

Bessie hesitated.

After all, why not? Maw Hoover would never have let her do anything like that—but Maw Hoover couldn't stop her from doing anything she liked now. Wanaka had told her what Zara had always said, that Maw Hoover couldn't make her stay, couldn't make her keep on working hard every day for nothing but her board. She had read about girls who had gone to the city and earned money, lots of money, without working any harder than she had always done. Perhaps could do that, too.

"You talk to Wanaka about that when she comes back," said Minnehaha, who guessed what Bessie was thinking. "You see her. She'll explain it to you. And you're going to be happy, Bessie. I'm sure of that. When people do right, and still aren't happy for a while, it's always made up to them some way. And usually when they do wrong they have to pay for it, some way or another. That's one of the things we learn in the Camp Fire."

"Here comes Wanaka now," said one of the other girls. "There's someone with her."

Bessie looked frightened.

"I don't want anyone from Hedgeville to see me," she said. "Do you suppose they're coming here?"

"Wanaka will come first. See, she's staying on the other side of the lake. It's a man. He's carrying her things. I'll paddle over for her in a canoe. I don't think the man will come with her, but you and Zara go into the tent there. Then you'll be all right. No one would ever think of your being here, or asking any questions."

But Bessie watched anxiously. She couldn't make out the face of the man with Wanaka, as she peered from the door of the tent, but if he was from Hedgeville he would know her. Everyone knew the girl at Hoovers', whose father and mother had deserted her. Bessie had long been one of the most interesting people in town to the farmers and the villagers, who had little to distract or amuse them.

"Stay quiet, Bessie," warned Minnehaha, as she stepped into the canoe. "You'll be all right if you're not seen. I'll bring Wanaka back right away."

With swift, sure strokes, Minnehaha sent the canoe skimming over the water. The other girls were busy in various ways. Some were in the tents, changing their clothes for bathing suits; some had gone into the woods to get fresh water from a spring. For the moment no one was in sight. And suddenly, out of a clear sky, as it seemed, disaster threatened. Clouds had been gathering for some time but the sun was still out, and there seemed no reason to fear any storm.

But now there was a sudden roughening of the smooth surface of the water; white caps were lashed up by a squall that broke with no warning at all. And Bessie, filled with horror, saw the canoe overturned by the wind. She saw, too, what eyes less quick would have missed—that the paddle, released from Minnehaha's grasp as the boat upset, struck her on the head.

For a moment Bessie stood rooted to the spot in terror. And then, when Minnehaha did not appear, swimming, Bessie acted. Forgotten was the danger that she would be discovered—her fear of the man on the other side of the lake. Wanaka might not have seen, and there was no time to lose. The accident had occurred in the middle of the lake, and Bessie, rushing to the beach, pushed off a canoe and began to drive it toward the other canoe, floating quietly now, bottom up. The squall had passed already.

Bessie had never been in a canoe before that day. She made clumsy work of the paddling. But fear for Minnehaha and the need of reaching her at once made up for any lack of skill. Somehow she reached the spot. By that time the other girls had seen what was going on, and help was coming quickly. Some swam and some were in one of the other canoes. But Bessie, catching a one of the most interesting people in town to the farmers and the villagers, who had little to distract or amuse them.

"Stay quiet, Bessie," warned Minnehaha, as she stepped into the canoe. "You'll be all right if you're not seen. I'll bring Wanaka back right away."

With swift, sure strokes, Minnehaha sent the canoe skimming over the water. The other girls were busy in various ways. Some were in the tents, changing their clothes for bathing suits; some had gone into the woods to get fresh water from a spring. For the moment no one was in sight. And suddenly, out of a clear sky, as it seemed, disaster threatened. Clouds had been gathering for some time but the sun was still out, and there seemed no reason to fear any storm.

But now there was a sudden roughening of the smooth surface of the water; white caps were lashed up by a squall that broke with no warning at all. And Bessie, filled with horror, saw the canoe overturned by the wind. She saw, too, what busy with Minnehaha, who soon showed signs of returning consciousness. So Bessie did not see or hear what was going on outside.

For the man who had been standing with Wanaka on the other shore had seen Bessie, and he had known her. No wonder, since it was Paw Hoover himself, from whom Wanaka had bought fresh vegetables for the camp. He had insisted on helping her to carry them out, although Wanaka, thinking of Bessie and Zara, had told him she needed no help. But she could not shake him off, and on the way he had told her about the exciting happenings of the previous day, of which, she told him, she had already heard in the village.

"By Godfrey!" said Paw Hoover, as he saw the rescue of Minnehaha, "that young one's got pluck, so she has! And, what's more, Miss, I've a suspicion I've seen her before!"

Wanaka said nothing, but smiled. What Paw Hoover had told her had done more to confirm the truth of Bessie's story than all the talk she had heard in Hedgeville. She liked the old farmer—and she wondered what he meant to do. He didn't leave her long in doubt.

"I'll just go over with you," he said, "if you'll make out to ferry me back here again."

And Wanaka dared not refuse.

"Had an idea you was askin' a lot of questions," said Paw Hoover, with a chuckle. "Got lots of ideas I keep to myself—'specially at home. An' say, if that's Bessie, I want to see her."

Wanaka saw that there was some plan in his mind, and she knew that to try to ward him off would be dangerous. There was nothing to prevent him from returning, later, with Weeks or anyone else.

"Bessie!" she called. "Can you come out here a minute?"

And Bessie, coming out, came face to face with Paw Hoover! She stared at him, frightened and astonished, but she held her ground. And Paw Hoover's astonishment was as great as her own. This was a new Bessie he had never seen before. She was neatly dressed now in one of Ayu's blue skirts and white blouses, and one of the girls had done up her hair in a new way.

"Well, I swan!" he said. "You've struck it rich, ain't you, Bessie? Aimin' to run away and leave us?"

Bessie couldn't answer, but Wanaka spoke up.

"You haven't any real hold on her, Mr. Hoover," she said.

"That's right, that's right!" said Paw Hoover. "I cal'late you've had a hard time once in a while, Bessie. An' I don't believe you ever set that shed afire on purpose. If you hadn't jumped into the water after that other girl I'd never have suspicioned you was here, Bessie. You stay right with these young ladies, if they'll have you. I'll not say a word. An' if you ever get into trouble, you write to me—see?"

He looked at her, and sighed. Then he beckoned to her, and took her aside.

"Maw's right set on havin' her own way, Bessie," he said. "But she's my wife, an' she's a good one, an' if she makes mistakes, I've got to let her have her way. Reckon I've made enough on 'em myself. Here, you take this. I guess you've earned it, right enough. That fire didn't do no real damage—nothin' we can't fix up in a day or two."

Bessie's eyes filled with tears. Paw Hoover was simply proving again what she had always known—that he was a really good and kindly man. She longed to tell him that she hadn't set the barn on fire, that it had been Jake. But she knew he would find it hard to believe that of his son, and that, even if he took her word for it, the knowledge would be a blow. And it would do her no good, so she said nothing of that.

"Thank you, Paw," she said. "You always were good to me. I'll never forget you, and sometime I'll come back to see you and all the others. Good-bye!"

"Good-bye, Bessie," he said. "You be a good girl and you'll get along all right. And you stick to Miss Mercer there. She'll see that you get along."

Not until he had gone did Bessie open her hand and look at the crumpled bill that Paw Hoover had left in it. And then, to her amazed delight, she saw that it was a five-dollar note—more money than she had ever had. She showed it to Wanaka.

"I oughtn't to take it," she said. "He thinks I burned his woodshed and—"

"But you know you didn't, and I think maybe he knows it, too," said Wanaka, "You needn't think anything of taking that money. You've worked hard enough to earn a lot more than that. Now I've found out that what you told me was just right. I knew it all the time, but I made sure. Bessie, how would you and Zara like to stay with us, and come back to the city when we go? I'll be able to find some way to look after you. You can find work to do that won't be so hard, and you can study, too."

"Oh, I'd love that, Wanaka," For the first time Bessie used the name freely. "And can we be Camp Fire Girls?"

"You certainly can," said Wanaka.

CHAPTER V

AN ALARM IN THE NIGHT

Bessie, overjoyed by Paw Hoover's kindness and his promise to do nothing toward having her taken back to Hedgeville, spent the rest of the afternoon happily. Indeed, she was happier than she could ever remember having been before. But her joy was dashed when, a little while before supper, she came upon Zara, crying bitterly. Zara had gone off by herself, and Bessie, going to the spring for water, came upon her.

"Why, Zara, whatever is the matter? We're all right now," cried Bessie.

"I—I know that, Bessie! But I'm so worried about my father!"

"Oh, Zara, what a selfish little beast I am! I was so glad to think that I wasn't going to be taken back that I forgot all about him. But cheer up! I'm sure he's done nothing wrong, and I'll talk to Wanaka, and see if there isn't something I can do or that she can do. I believe she can do anything if she makes up her mind she will."

"Did she hear anything about him in Hedgeville?"

"Only what we knew before, Zara, that they'd come for him and taken him to the city. But Wanaka said she was sure that it is only gossip, and that he needn't be afraid. And we're going to the city, too, you know, so you'll be able to see him."

"Will I, Bessie? Then that won't be so bad. If I could only talk to him I'm sure it would seem better. And you must be right—they can't punish a man when he hasn't done anything wrong, can they?"

"Of course not," said Bessie, laughing.

"In the country where we came from they do, sometimes," said Zara, thoughtfully. "My father has told me about things like that."

"In Italy, Zara?"

"Yes. We're not Italians, really, but that's where we lived."

"But you don't remember anything about that, do you?"

"No, but I've been told all about it. We used to live in a white house, on a hillside. And there were lemon trees and olive trees growing there, and all sorts of beautiful things. And you could look out over the blue sea, and see the boats sailing, and away off there was a great mountain."

"I should think you'd want to go back there, Zara. It must have been beautiful."

"Oh, I've always wanted to see that place, Bessie. Sometimes, my father says, the mountain, would smoke, and fire would come out of it, and the ground would shake. But it never hurt the place where we lived."

"That must have been a volcano, Zara."

"Yes, that's what he used to call it."

"Why did you come over here?"

"Because my father was always afraid over there. There were some bad men who hated him, and he said that if he stayed there they would hurt him. And he heard that over here everyone was welcome, and one man was as good as another. But he wasn't, or they never seemed to think so, if he was."

Bessie looked very thoughtful.

"This is the finest country in the world, Zara," she said. "I've heard that, and I've read it in books, too. But I guess that things go wrong here sometimes. You see, it's this way. Just think of Jake Hoover."

"But I don't want to think about him! I want to forget him!"

"Well, Jake Hoover explains what I'm thinking about. He's an American, but that isn't the reason he was so mean to us. He'd be mean anywhere, no matter whether he was an American or what. He just can't help it. And I think he'll get over it, anyhow."

"There you go, Bessie! He's made all this trouble for you, and you're standing up for him already."

"No, I'm not. But what trouble has he made for me, Zara? I'm going to be happier than I ever was back there in Hedgeville—and if it hadn't been for him I'd still be there, and I'd be chopping wood or something right now."

"But he didn't mean to make you happier, Bessie. He thought he could get you punished for something he'd done."

"Well, I wasn't, so why should I be angry at him, Zara? Even if he did mean to be nasty, he wasn't."

"But suppose he'd hurt you some way, without meaning to at all? Would you be angry at him then for hurting you, when he didn't mean to do it?"

"Of course not—just because he didn't mean to."

"Well, then," said Zara, triumphantly, "you ought to be angry now, if it's what one means to do, and not what one does that counts. I would be."

Bessie laughed. For once Zara seemed to have trapped her and beaten her in an argument.

"But I don't like to be angry, and to feel revengeful," she said. "It hurts me more than it does the other person. When anything happens that isn't nice it only bothers you as long as you keep on thinking about it, Zara. Suppose someone threw a stone at you, and hit you?"

"It would hurt me—and I'd want to throw it back."

"But then suppose the stone was thrown, and it didn't hit you, and you didn't even know it had been thrown, you wouldn't be angry then, would you?"

"Why, how could I be, Bessie, if I didn't know anything about it?"

"Well, don't you see how it worked out, Zara? If you refuse to notice the mean things people do when they don't succeed in hurting you, it's just as if you didn't know anything about it, isn't it? And if the stone was thrown, and you saw it, and knew who'd thrown it, you'd be angry—but you could get over it by just making up your mind to forget it, and acting as if they'd never done it at all."

Zara didn't answer for a minute. She was thinking that over.

"I guess you're right, Bessie," she said, finally. "That is the best way to do. When I get angry I get all hot inside, and I feel dreadful. I'm going to try not to lose my temper any more."

"You'll be a lot happier if you do that," said Bessie. "Now, let's get back to the fire. I've got this water, and they must be waiting for it."

So Zara, happy again, and laughing now, helped Bessie with the pail of water, and they went back to the fire together. Everyone was busy, each with some appointed task. Two of the girls were spreading knives and forks, and laying out cups and dishes in a great circle near the water, since all the meals were eaten Indian fashion, sitting on the ground. Others, who had been fishing, were displaying their catch, and cleaning the gleaming trout, soon to be cooked with crisp bacon, and to form the chief dish of the evening meal.

Wanaka smiled at them as the two girls appeared with the water.

"You're making a good start as Camp Fire Girls," she told them. "We all try to help. Later on, if you like, I'll give you a lesson in cooking."

Bessie smiled, but said nothing. And presently she called to Zara and disappeared with her in the woods.

"I want to give them a surprise, Zara," she said. "There's quite a long time yet before supper. And I saw an apple tree when I was walking through the woods. Let's go and get some of them."

Zara was quite willing, and in half an hour or less the two girls were back in camp with a good load of apples. Then Bessie spoke to Wanaka when the Guardian was alone for the moment.

"May I have some flour and sugar?" she said.

Wanaka looked at her curiously, but gave her what she wanted. And Bessie, finding a smooth white board, was soon busy rolling pastry. Then when she had made a great deep dish pie, and filled it with the apples, which Zara, meanwhile, had pared and cut, Bessie set to work on what was the most difficult part of her task. First she dug out a hole in the ground and made a fire, small, but very hot, and, in a short time, with the aid of two flat stones, she had constructed a practicable outdoor oven, in which the heat of the embers and cinders was retained by shutting out the air with earth. Then the pie was put in and covered at once, so that no heat could escape, and Bessie, saying nothing about what she had done, went back to help the others.

Obeying the unwritten rule of the Camp Fire, which allows the girls to work out their ideas unaided if they possibly can, so as to encourage self-reliance and independence, Wanaka did not ask her what she had done. But when the meal was over Bessie slipped away, while Wanaka was serving out some preserves, and returned in a moment, bearing her pie—nobly browned, with crisp, flaky crust.

"I've only made one pie like this before and I never used that sort of an oven," she said, shyly. "So I don't know if it's very good. But I thought I would try it."

Bessie, however, need not have worried about the quality of that pie. The rapidity with which it disappeared was the best possible evidence of its goodness, and Wanaka commended her before all the girls, who were willing enough to join the leader in singing Bessie's praises.

"My, but that was good!" said Minnehaha. "I wish I could make a pie like that! My pastry is always heavy. Will you show me how when we get home, Bessie?"

"Indeed I will!" promised Bessie.

And that night, after a spell of singing and story telling about the great fire on the beach, Bessie and Zara went to bed with thoughts very different from those they had had the night before.

"Aren't they good to us, Zara?" said Bessie.

"They're simply wonderful," said Zara, with shining eyes. "And Wanaka talked to me about my father. She says she has a friend in the city who's a lawyer, and that as soon as we get back she'll speak to him, and get him to see that he is fairly treated. I feel ever so much better."

The voices of the girls all about them, laughing and singing as they made ready for the night, and the kindly words of Wanaka, made a great contrast to their loneliness of the night before. Then everything had seemed black and dismal. They hadn't known what they were going to do, or what was to happen to them; they had been hungry and tired, and with no prospect of breakfast when they got up. But now they had more friends, gained in one wonderful day, than they had made before in all their lives, and Wanaka had promised to see that in the future there should always be someone to guide them and see that no one abused them any more. No wonder that they looked on the bright camp fire, symbol of all the happiness that had come to them, with happy eyes. And they listened in delight as the girls gathered, just before they went to bed, and sang the good-night song:

"Lay me to sleep in sheltering flame,

Oh, Master of the Hidden Fire.

Wash pure my heart and cleanse for me

My soul's desire.

In flame of sunrise bathe my mind,

Oh, Master of the Hidden Fire,

That when I wake, clear eyed may be

My soul's desire."

And so, with the flames' light flickering before them, Bessie and Zara went to sleep sure of happiness and companionship when they awoke in the morning, with the first rays of the rising sun shining into the tents.

But Bessie was to awake before that. She lay near the door of one of the tents, which she shared with Zara, Minnehaha, and two other girls, and she awoke suddenly, coming at once to full consciousness, as anyone who had been brought up with Maw Hoover to wake her every morning was pretty certain to do at any unusual sound. For a moment, so deep was the silence, she thought that she had been deceived. In the distance an owl called; much nearer, there was an answer. A light wind rustled in the trees, stirring the leaves gently as it moved. Looking out, she saw that a faint, silvery sheen still bathed the ground outside, showing that the moon, which had risen late, was not yet set.

And then the sound that had awakened her came again—a curious, hoarse call, given in imitation of a whip-poor-will, but badly done. No bird had uttered that cry, and Bessie, country bred, listening intently, knew it.

Silently she rose and slipped on moccasins that belonged to Minnehaha, and a dress. And then, making no more noise than a cat would have done, she crept to the opening in the front of the tent and peeped out. For Bessie had recognized the author of that imitation of the bird's call, and she knew that there was mischief afoot.

Still intent on keeping the alarm she felt from the others, until she knew whether there was a real cause for it, Bessie slipped out of the tent and into the shadow of the trees. The camp fire still burned, flickering in the darkness, and making great, weird shadows, as the light fell upon the trees. It had been built up and banked before the camp went to sleep, and in the morning it would still be burning, although faintly, ready for the first careful attentions of the appointed Wood-Gatherers, whose duty it was to see that the fire did not die.

Bessie, fearing that she might be spied upon, had to keep in the darkness, and she twisted and turned from the trunk of one tree to the next, bending over close to the ground when she had to cross an open space where firelight or moonbeams might reveal her to watching eyes.

And now and again, crudely given, as crudely answered, from further down the lake, the call of the mock whip-poor-will guided her in her quest. And Bessie, plucking up all the courage she could muster, still trembled slightly, more from nervousness than from actual fear, for she knew whose voice it was that was imitating the plaintive bird—Jake Hoover's!

All Hedgeville, as she well knew, must know that this camp of girls was at the lake—and it would be just like Jake and some of the bullying, reckless crowd of boys that he made his chief friends, to think that it would be a fine joke to play some tricks on the sleeping camp, and alarm these girls who were trying to enjoy themselves with outdoor life, just as if they had been boys. Bessie, setting her teeth, determined that they shouldn't succeed, that in some fashion she would turn the joke on them.

Gradually she drew nearer to the sound, and she made up her mind, thankfully, that she had waked in time, before all the jokers had arrived. She had snatched up a sheet as she left the camp, without a clear idea of what she meant to do with it, but now, as she stole among the trees, a dim figure, flitting from one dark place to the next, a wild idea formed in her mind.

It was risky—but Bessie was not timid. If Jake Hoover caught her—well, she knew what that would mean. He would not spare her, as his father had done, and there would be trouble for her, and for Zara and, worst of all, for Wanaka and her other new friends. And there was another danger. It might not, after all, be Jake Hoover that she heard.

At the Hoovers' she had heard stories of tramps and wandering gypsies, and she had been warned, whenever there was a report that any such vagrants were about, to keep off the roads and stay near the house. Jake, after all, could only betray her to his mother and the others who were after her, but a tramp or a gypsy might do far worse than that. But, though the solitude and the darkness were enough to frighten people older and stronger than Bessie, she kept on. And at last, before her, she heard footsteps tramping down the dry leaves and branches, and she heard a murmur of voices, too.

At once part of her fears fled, for it was Jake Hoover's voice that came to her ears.

"Ha-ha!" he was laughing. "Gee, it took you fellers long enough to git here. But, say, boys, won't we have some fun with them girls? Actin' up just like they was boys, sleepin' out in the woods an' pretendin' they're as brave as anythin'. I saw that one that bought a lot of truck from Paw to-day. Bet she'll scream as loud as any of them."

"Bet she will," said another voice. "Say, Jake, we won't hurt 'em none, will we? Jest throw a scare into them, like?"

"Sure, that's all!"

"'Cause I wouldn't want to hurt 'em none. They're jest girls, after all."

"All we'll do will be just to get around them tents an' start yellin' all at once—an' I'll bet they'll come a-runnin'. Ha-ha!"

But the laugh was frozen on his lips. As he spoke he looked behind him, warned by a faint sound—and his hair rose. For waving its arms wildly, a figure, all in white, was running toward him. As it came it made strange, unearthly sounds—horrid noises, such as Jake had never heard.

For a moment Jake and the two boys with him stood rooted to the spot, paralyzed with fear. Then they yelled together, and, the sound of their own voices seeming to release their imprisoned feet, turned and ran wildly, not knowing where they were going.

They tripped over roots, fell, then stumbled to their feet again, and continued their flight, shrieking. And behind them the ghost, weak with laughter, collapsed on a fallen tree trunk and laughed silently as they fled—for the ghost that had frightened these bold raiders was only Bessie, wrapped in the sheet she had so luckily snatched up when they had given her the alarm.

CHAPTER VI

A PIECE OF BAD LUCK

Bessie laughed until she cried as the bold raiders who had been so sure that they could scare the camp of girls dashed madly off. She could hear them long after they had vanished from sight, crying out in their fear, plunging among the trees, but gradually the sounds grew fainter, and Bessie, sure that they need fear no more disturbance from Jake Hoover and his brave companions, set out on her return to the camp. This time she had no need of the precautions she had taken as she crept in the direction of the disturbing sounds, and she made no effort to conceal herself.

Wanaka was outside, looking about anxiously, when Bessie came again into the firelight. Always a light sleeper, and especially so when she was responsible for the safety of the girls who were in her charge, Eleanor Mercer had waked at first of Bessie's terrifying shrieks, almost as frightened, for the moment, as Jake himself. She had risen at once, and a glance in the various tents, where the girls still lay sound asleep, showed her that Bessie alone was missing.

Naturally enough, she could not guess the meaning of the outcry. The cries of the frightened jokers puzzled her, and there was nothing about the din that Bessie made to enable the Guardian to recognize the voice of her newest recruit. But she had realized, too, that to go out in the woods in search of Bessie and of an explanation, was not likely to do much good. Her duty, too, was with the girls who remained, and she could only wait, wondering. She greeted Bessie with a glad cry when she saw her.

"Oh, I'm so glad!" she exclaimed. "But what are you doing with that sheet? And—why, you're crying!"

"I'm not—really," said Bessie. "But I laughed so hard that it made the tears come—that's all, Wanaka."

Then she told her story, and Wanaka had to laugh, too. She was greatly relieved.

"But you ought to have called me, Bessie," she said. "That's why I'm here, you know—to look out for things when there seems to be any danger, or anything you girls don't quite understand."

"But I wasn't quite sure, you see," said Bessie. "And if it had really been a bird, it would have been awfully foolish to wake everyone up just because I thought I heard something."

"You'll be able to win a lot of honors easily, Bessie, when you come into the Camp Fire. That's one of the things the girls do—they learn the calls of the birds, and to describe them and all sorts of things about the trees and the flowers. You must know a lot of them already."

"I guess everyone does who's lived in the country. Some people can imitate a bird so it would almost fool another bird—but not Jake. He's stupid."

"Yes, and like most people who try to frighten others, he's a coward, too, Bessie. He showed that to-night."

"I'm not afraid of him any more. If I'd known before how easy it was to frighten him I'd have done it. Then he'd have let me alone, probably."

"Well, you go to bed now, and get to sleep again. And try to forget about Jake and all the other people who have been unkind to you. Remember that you're safe with us now. We'll look after you."

"I know that, and I can't tell you how good it makes me feel."

Wanaka laughed then, to herself.

"I say we'll look after you," she said, still smiling. "But so far it looks more as if you were going to look after us. You saved Minnehaha in the lake—and to-night you saved all the girls from being frightened. But we'll have to begin doing our share before long."

"As if you hadn't done a lot more for me already than I'll ever be able to repay!" said Bessie. "And I know it, too. Please be sure of that. Good-night."

"Good-night, Bessie."

In the morning Bessie and Zara woke with the sun shining in their faces, and for a long minute they lay quiet, staring out at the dancing water, and trying to realize all that happened since they had said good-bye to Hedgeville.

"Just think, Zara, it's only the day before yesterday that all those things happened, and it seems like ever so long to me."

"It does to me, too, Bessie. But I'll be glad when we get away from here. It's awfully close."

"And, Zara, Jake Hoover was around here last night!"

"Does he know you're here? Was that why he came?"

"No," said Bessie, laughing again at the memory of the ghost. And she told Zara what had happened.

"He won't come around again at night, but it would be just like him to snoop around here in the daytime, Bessie."

"I hadn't thought of that, Zara. But he might. If he stops to think and realizes that someone turned his own trick against him, or if he tells someone, and they laugh at him, he'll want to get even. I'd certainly hate to have him see one of us."

But their fears were groundless. For, as soon as breakfast was over, Wanaka called all the girls together.

"We're going to move," she said. "I know we meant to stay here longer, but Bessie and Zara will be happier if we're somewhere else. So we will go on today, instead of waiting. And I've a pleasant surprise for you, too, I think. No, I won't tell you about it now. You'll have to wait until you see it. Hurry up and clean camp now, and begin packing. We want to start as soon as we can."

Bessie was amazed to see how complete the arrangements for packing were. Everything seemed to have its place, and to be so made that it could go into the smallest space imaginable. The tents were taken down, divided into single sections that were not at all heavy, and everything else had been made on the same plan.

"But how about the canoes?" asked Bessie. "We can't carry those with us, can we?"

"I've often carried one over a portage—a short walk from one lake to the next in the woods," said Minnehaha, laughing. "It's a lot easier than it looks. Once you get it on your back, it balances so easily that it isn't hard at all. And up in the woods the guides have boats that they carry that way for miles, and they say they're easier to handle than a heavy pack. But those boats are very light."

"But we'll leave them here, anyhow," said another girl. "They don't belong to us. They were just lent to us by some people from the city who come here to camp every summer. They own this land, too, and they let us use it."

And then Bessie saw, as the first canoe was brought in, the clever hiding-place that had been devised for the boats. They were dragged up, and carried into the woods a little way, and there a couple of fallen trees had been so arranged that they made a shelter for the canoes. A few boards were spread between the trunks, and covered with earth and branches so it seemed that shrubbery had grown up over the place where the canoes lay.

"In the winter, of course, the people that own them take them away where they'll be safe. But they leave them out like that most of the summer. Some of them come here quite often, and it would be a great nuisance to have to drag the canoes along every time they come and go."

Long before noon everything was ready, and Wanaka, who had gone away for a time, returned.

"You and Zara look so different that I don't believe anyone would recognize either of you," she told Bessie. "You look just like the rest of the girls. So, even if we should meet anyone who knows you, I think you'd be safe enough."

"Not if it was Maw Hoover," said Zara so earnestly that Wanaka laughed, although she felt that there was something pathetic about Zara's fear of the farmer's wife, too.

"Well, we're not going to meet her, anyhow, Zara. And she'd never expect to find you and Bessie among us, anyhow. We aren't going across the lake and over to the main road. We're going right through the woods to the next valley. It's going to be a long day's trip, but it's cool, and I think a good long tramp will do us all good."

"That's fine," said Bessie. "No one over there will know anything about us. Is that why we made so many sandwiches and things like that—so that we could eat our lunch on the way?"

"Yes, and we'll build a fire and have something hot, too. Now you can watch us put out the fire."

"I hate to see it go out," said Zara. "I love the fire."

"We all do, but we must never leave a fire without someone to tend it. Fire is a great servant, but we must use it properly. And a little fire, even this one of ours, might start a bad blaze in the woods here if we left it behind us."

Bessie nodded wisely.

"We had an awful bad fire here two or three years ago. It was just before Zara came out here. Someone was out in the woods hunting, or something like that, and they left a fire, and the wind came up and set the trees on fire. It burned for three or four days, and all the men in the town had to turn out to save some of the places near the woods."

"Almost all the big fires in the forests start because someone is careless just like that, Bessie. They don't mean any harm—but they don't stop to think."

Then all the girls gathered about the fire, and each in turn did her part in stamping out the glowing embers. They sang as they did this duty, and Bessie felt again the curious thrill that had stirred her when she had heard the good-night song the evening before.

"I know what it is that is so splendid about the Camp Fire Girls, Zara," she said, suddenly. "They belong to one another, and they do things together. That's what counts—that's why they look so happy. We've never had anything to belong to, you and I, anything like this. Don't you see what I mean?"

"Yes, I do, Bessie. And that's what makes it seem so easy when they work. They're doing things together, and each of them has something to do at the same time that all the others are working, too."

"Why, I just loved washing the dishes this morning," said Bessie, smiling at the thought. "I never felt like that before, when Maw Hoover was always at me to do them, so that I could hurry up and do something else when I got through. And I did them faster here, too—much faster. Just because I enjoyed it, and it seemed like the most natural thing to do."

"I always did feel that way, but then I only worked for myself and my father," said Zara.

Then the walk through the cool, green woods began. The girls started out in Indian file, but presently the trail broadened, so that they could walk two or three abreast. It was not long before they came into country that Bessie had never seen, well as she knew the woods near the Hoover farmhouse.

Wanaka, careful lest too steady a walk should tire the girls, called a halt at least once an hour, and, when the trail led up hill, oftener. And at each halt one girl or another, who had been detailed at the last stop, reported on the birds and wild animals she had seen since the last check, and, when she had done, all the others were called on to tell if they had seen any that she had missed.

"It's just like a game, isn't it?" said Zara. "I think it's great fun!"

The halt for lunch was made after they had come out of the woods, by the side of a clear spring. They were on a bluff, high above a winding country road, with a path worn by the feet of thirsty passersby who knew of the spring, and some thoughtful person had piped the water down to a big trough where horses could drink. But they could not, from the place where the fire had been made, see the road or the carriages.

"I don't think anyone will come along looking for you," Wanaka told Bessie, "but if we stay out of sight we'll surely be on the safe side."

Suddenly, as they were about to sit down, Zara cried out.

"My handkerchief!" she said. "It's gone—and I had it just before we crossed the road. I must have dropped it there. I'll go back and see."

"I'll go with you," cried Bessie, jumping up. But before she could move, Zara, laughing, had dashed off, and Bessie dropped back to her place with a smile.

"She's as quick as a flash," she said. "She always could beat me in a race. There's no use in my going after her."

But, even as she spoke, a wild cry of terror reached their ears—that and the sound of a man's coarse laughter. Bessie started to her feet, her eyes staring in fright. And she led the rush of the whole party to the edge of the bluff.

Driving swiftly down the road away from Hedgeville was a runabout. And in it Bessie saw Zara, held fast by a big man whose back she recognized at once. It was Farmer Weeks!

"Oh, that's Farmer Weeks!" she cried "He'll get them to give Zara to him, and he'll beat her and treat her terribly."

Despairingly she made to run after the disappearing horse. But Wanaka checked her, gently.

"We must be careful—and slow," she said.

CHAPTER VII

A FRIEND IN NEED

"But we must do something, really we must, Miss Eleanor!" cried Bessie. "I must, I mean. Zara trusted me, and if I don't help her now, just think of what will happen."

"You must keep calm, Bessie, that's the first thing to think of. If you let yourself get excited and worked up you won't help Zara, and you'll only get into trouble yourself. You say she trusted you—now you must trust me a little. Tell me, first, just what this man will do and if he has any right at all to touch her."

"Why, he's the meanest man in town, Wanaka! He really is—everyone says so! None of the men would work for him in harvest time. They said he worked them to death and wouldn't give them enough to eat."

"Yes, but why should he pick Zara up that way and carry her off?"

"Because he wants to make her work for him. He's awfully rich, and Paw Hoover said he'd lent money to so many men in the village and all around that they had to do just what he told them, or he'd sell their land and their horses and cattle. And he said he'd make the people at the poor-farm bind Zara over to him and then she'd have to work for him until she was twenty-one, just for her board."

"That's pretty serious, Bessie. I'm sure he wouldn't be a good guardian, but if he had such influence over the men, maybe they wouldn't stop to think about that."

She was silent for a minute, thinking hard.

"Where was he going with her, Bessie? He seemed to be driving away from Hedgeville."

"Yes, he was. I suppose he was going over to Zebulon. That's the county seat, and he goes over there quite often. Almost every time they hold court, I guess. Paw Hoover said he was a mighty bad neighbor, always getting into lawsuits."

"Well, I think I'd better go to Zebulon. If I talk to him, perhaps I can make him give Zara up. How far is it, Bessie?"

"Only about two miles. But if you go, can't I go with you?"

"I think I'd better go alone, Bessie. If he saw you, he might try to take you back to the Hoovers, you know. No, I'll go alone. If it's only two miles, it won't take me long to walk there, and I can get someone to drive me back. Girls!"

They crowded about her.

"I'm going away for a little while. You are to stay here and wait for me. And keep close together. I'll get back as soon as I can. And while I'm gone you can clear up the mess we made with luncheon—when you've finished it, I mean. Now, you'd better hurry up and eat it. I won't wait."

And the guardian hurried off, determined to rescue Zara from the clutches of the old miser who was so anxious to make her work for him, because he saw a chance to get a good deal for nothing, or almost nothing. If the general opinion about Silas Weeks was anywhere near true, it would cost him mighty little to satisfy himself that he was keeping faith with the county and giving Zara, in return for her services, good board, lodging, and clothing.

Bessie watched Wanaka go off, and she tried to convince herself that everything would be all right. But, strong as was the faith she already had in Miss Mercer, she knew the ways of Silas Weeks too well to be really confident. And she couldn't get rid of the feeling that she, and no one else, was responsible for Zara. It was because of her that Zara had come away, and Bessie felt that she should make sure, herself, that Zara didn't have cause to regret the decision.

And then, suddenly, too, another thought struck her. What if she had, without intention, misled Miss Eleanor? Suppose Farmer Weeks didn't go to Zebulon at all? It was possible, for Bessie remembered now that three-quarters of a mile or so along the road was a crossroad that would lead him, should he turn there, back to Hedgeville.

With the thought Bessie could no longer remain still. She knew the roads, and she determined that she must at least find out where Zara had been taken. She might not be able to help her herself, but she could get the news, the true news, for those who could. And, saying nothing to any of the other girls, lest they should want to come with her, she slipped off silently.

She did not descend to the road. If one farmer from Hedgeville had passed already, others might follow in his wake, and Bessie was fiercely determined not to let anything check her or interfere with her until she knew what had become of Zara.

So, although she might have been able to travel faster by the road, Bessie stayed above, and hurried along, making the best progress she could, although the going was rough. She could see, without being seen. If anyone who threatened her liberty came along, she could hide easily enough behind a tree or a clump of bushes.

At the crossroad she hesitated. She wasn't sure that Farmer Weeks had turned off. He might very well, as she had thought at first, have been on his way to Zebulon.

"What a stupid I am!" she thought in a moment, however. "Of course I ought to take the crossroad! If he's gone to Zebulon Wanaka will find him, and if he hasn't, he must have gone this way. If I turn off here, there'll be someone after him, no matter which way he's gone."

So, still keeping to the side of the road, she followed the pointer on the signboard which said, "Hedgeville, six miles."

About a mile and a half from the crossroads the road Bessie was now following crossed a railroad, and as she neared that spot she moved as carefully as she could, for a suspicion that gave her a ray of hope was rising in her mind. At the railroad crossing there was a little settlement and an inn that was very popular with automobilists. And Bessie thought it was possible that Farmer Weeks might have stopped there. Miser as he was, he was fond of good food, and, since he was his own cook most of the time when he was at home, he didn't get much of it except when he was away, as he was now. Bessie had heard Maw Hoover sneer at him more than once for the way he hinted for an invitation to dinner or supper.

"Old skinflint!" Bessie had heard Maw say. "I notice he has a way of forgettin' anythin' he wants to tell Paw till jest before meal time. Then he comes over post haste, and nothin'll do but Paw's got to stand out there listenin' to him, when all he wants, really, is to have me ring the bell, so's Paw'll have to ask him to stay."

Even in her sorrow at Zara's plight, Bessie couldn't help laughing at the remembrance of those times. But then the smoke of the inn came in sight, and Bessie forgot everything but the need of caution. If Farmer Weeks were there, he must on no account see her. That would end any chance she had of helping Zara.

She crept through a grove of trees that surrounded the inn, to work up behind it. In the rear, as she knew, were the stables, and the place where the automobiles of the guests were kept. She wanted to get a look at the horses and carriages that were tied in the shed for she would know Farmer Weeks' rig anywhere, she was sure. But she had to be careful, for the inn was a busy spot, and around the horses and the autos, especially, were lots of men, working, smoking, loafing—and any one of them, Bessie felt sure, was certain to question her if they saw her prowling about.

She got behind the shed, and then she had to work along to the end farthest from the direction of the road she had left, since, at the near end, a group of men were sitting down and eating their lunch. But, with the shed full of horses making plenty of noise, to screen her movements, that wasn't so difficult. Bessie managed it all right, and, when she got to the far end, and had a chance to peep at the horses, her heart leaped joyfully, for she saw within a few feet of her Farmer Weeks' horse and buggy, the buggy sadly in need of paint and repairs, and the harness a fair indication of the miserly nature of its owner, since it was patched in a dozen places and tied together with string in a dozen others.

"Well, I know that much, anyhow!" said Bessie to herself. "He didn't take her to Zebulon, and he can't have done anything yet. I don't believe he's got any right to keep her that way, not unless the people at the poor-farm give him the right to take her. Zara hasn't done anything—it isn't as if she'd been arrested, and were running away from that."

Suddenly Bessie started with alarm. She had drawn back among the trees to hide while she tried to think out the best course of action for her to take, and she heard someone moving quite close to her. But then, as the one who had frightened her came into view, she smiled, for it was only a small boy, very dirty and red of face, his white clothes soiled, but looking thoroughly happy, just the same.

"Hello!" he said, staring at her.

"Hello, yourself! Where did you come from? And wherever did you get all that dirt on yourself?"

"Oh, in the woods," said the small boy. "Say, my name's Jack Roberts, and my pop owns that hotel there. What's your name? Do you like cherries? Can you climb a tree? Did you ever go out in the woods all alone? Can you swim?"

"My, my! One question at a time," laughed Bessie. "I love cherries. Have you got some?"

"Bet I have!" he said. The single answer to all his questions seemed to satisfy him thoroughly, and he pulled out a great handful of cherries from his straw hat, which he had been using for a basket.

"Here you are," he said. "Say, do you know that other girl?"

Bessie's heart leaped again. She felt that she had struck real luck at last.

"What other girl?" she asked, but even as she asked the question, her heart sank again. He couldn't mean Zara. How could he possibly know anything about her?

"She was dressed just like you," he said. "And she had black hair and her skin was dark. So she didn't look like you at all, you see. She was crying, too. Say, aren't those cherries good? Why don't you eat them?"

Bessie was so interested and excited when she heard him speak of Zara that she forgot to eat the cherries. But she saw that she had hurt his feelings by her neglect of his present, and she made amends at once. She ate several of them, and smacked her lips.

"They're splendid, Jack! They're the best I've eaten this year. I think you're lucky to be able to get them."

Jack was delighted.

"You come here again later on and I'll give you some of the best pears you ever tasted."

"Tell me some more about the girl, Jack—the other girl, with black hair. I think perhaps she's a friend of mine. Why was she crying?"

"I don't know but she was. She was going on terrible. And she was with her pop, I guess. So I s'pose she'd just been naughty, and he'd punished her."

"What makes you think that, Jack?"

"Oh, he came in, and he talked to my pop, and they both laughed and looked at her. He had her by the hand, and she didn't say anything—she just cried. And my pop says, 'Well, I've got just the place for her. Too bad to send her off without her dinner, but when they're bad they've got to be punished.' And he winked at her, but she didn't wink back."

"What happened then, Jack?"

"They put her up in my room. See, you can see it there, right over the tree with the branch torn off. See that branch? It was torn off in that storm yesterday."

"And didn't she have any dinner?"

"Oh, yes. My pop, he sent her some dinner, of course. He was just joking. That's why he winked at her. He'd never let anyone go hungry, my pop wouldn't!"

"What sort of looking man brought her here, Jack?"

"Oh, he—he was just a man. He had white hair, and eye-glasses. Say, that's his rig right there in the corner of the shed. I don't think much of it, do you?"

Bessie wondered what she should do. She liked Jack, and she was sure he would do anything he could for her. But he was only a little boy, and it seemed as if that would not be very much. But he was her only hope, and she decided to trust him.

"Jack," she said, soberly, "that is my friend, and I've been looking for her. And that old man isn't her father at all. He wants to make her do something horrid—something she doesn't want to do at all. And if she doesn't get away, I'm afraid he will, too."

"Say, I didn't like him when I first saw him! I'd hate to have him for a pop. Why doesn't she run away?"

"How can she, Jack?"

"Huh, that's just as easy! Why, I never go down the stairs at all, hardly, from my room. The branches of that big tree stick right over to the window, and it's awful easy to climb down."

"She could do that, too, Jack, but she doesn't know I'm here to help her. She'd think there wasn't any use getting down."

"Say, I'll climb up and tell her, if you like. Shall I?"

"Will you, really, Jack? And tell her Bessie is waiting here for her? Will you show her how to get down, and how to get here? And don't you think someone will see her?"

"No, an' if they do, they can't catch us. I've got a cave back here that's the peachiest hiding-place you ever saw! I'll show you. They'll never find you there. You just wait!"

He was off like a flash, and Bessie, terribly anxious, but hopeful, too, saw him run up the tree like a squirrel. Then the branches hid him from her, and she couldn't see what happened at the window. But before she had waited more than two minutes, although it seemed like hours to poor Bessie, Jack was in sight again, and behind him came Zara. She dropped easily to the ground, and ran toward Bessie, behind Jack, like a scared rabbit.

"Oh, Bessie, I'm so glad—so glad!" she cried. "I was so frightened—"

From the inn there was a shout of anger.

"Gee! He's found out already," cried Jack. "Come on! Don't be scared! I'll show you where to hide so he'll never find you. Run—run, just as fast as you can!"

And they were off, while Farmer Weeks shouted behind them.

CHAPTER VIII

THE SHELTER OF THE WOODS

For the first few minutes as they ran, the three of them were too busy to talk, and they needed their breath too much to be anxious to say anything. Jack, his little legs flying, covered ground at an astonishing pace. Zara had always been a speedy runner, and now, clutching Bessie's hand tightly, she helped her over some of the harder places.

They were running right into the woods, as it seemed to Bessie, and more than once, as she heard sounds of pursuit behind, she was frightened. It seemed to her impossible that little Jack, mean he never so well, could possibly enable them to escape from angry Farmer Weeks, who, for an old man, seemed to be keeping up astonishingly well in the race. But soon the noises behind them grew fainter, and it was not long before the ground began to rise sharply. Jack dropped to a walk, and the two girls, panting from the hard run, were not slow to follow his example.

"This is like playing Indians," said Jack, happily. "It's lots of fun—much better than playing by myself. Here's my cave."

"Don't you think we'd better go on, Bessie?" panted Zara. "We're ahead of them now, and they might find us here."

"No, I think we'd better stop right here. Would you ever know there was a cave here if Jack hadn't uncovered the entrance? And see, it's so wild that we'd have to stick to the path, and we don't know the way. I'm afraid they'd be sure to catch us sooner or later if we went on."

"Listen!" said Jack. "They're getting nearer again!"

And sure enough, they could hear the shouts of those who were following them, and the noise was getting louder. Bessie hesitated no longer, but pushed Zara before her into the cave. Jack followed them.

"See," he said, "I can pull those branches over, and they'll never see the mouth of the cave. They'll think these are just bushes growing here. Isn't it a bully place? I've played it was a smuggler's cave, and all sorts of things, but it never was as good fun as this."

"Just think that way," said Bessie to poor Zara, who was trembling like a leaf. "When we get back with the girls, we'll think this is just good fun—a fine adventure. So cheer up, we're safe now."

"But how will we ever get back to them, even if they don't catch us now?" asked Zara. "We'll be seen when we go out, won't we?"

"No, indeed," said Bessie. "I'll bet Jack's thought about that, haven't you, Jack?"

"You bet!" he said, proudly. "They'll go by, and they'll keep on for a long way, and then they'll think they've gone so far that a girl couldn't ever have done it. And then they'll decide they've missed her, and they'll turn around and come back again, and hunt around near the hotel. And when they do that—"

"Hush!" said Bessie. "Here they come! Keep quiet, now, both of you! Don't even breathe hard—and don't sneeze, whatever you do!"

And then, lying down close to one another, at full length on the floor of the cave, which Jack, for his play, had covered with soft branches of evergreen trees, they peeped out through the leafy covering of the cave while Farmer Weeks went by, snorting and puffing angrily, like some wild animal, his eyes straight ahead. He never looked at the cave, or in their direction, but the next man, one employed about the hotel, seemed to have his eyes fixed directly on the branches. Bessie thought he looked suspicious. She was sure that he had spied the device, and was about to call to Farmer Weeks. But, when he was still a few feet off, he tripped over a root, and sprawled on his face, and, if he had ever really had any suspicions at all, the fall seemed to drive them from his mind effectually. He picked himself up, laughing, since the fall had not hurt him, and, after he had shouted back a warning to two men who followed him, he went on, dusting himself off.

The root had been good to the fugitives, sure enough, for the men who followed kept their eyes on the ground, looking out for it, since they had no desire to share the tumble of the man in front, and neither of them so much as looked at the cave.

"My, but they're brave men!" said Jack. "Three of them, all to chase one little girl!"

Zara, her fears somewhat relieved, laughed as she looked at her rescuer.

"I'm bigger than you are," she said, smiling.

"Yes, but you're a girl," said Jack, in a lordly fashion that would have made Bessie laugh if she hadn't been afraid of hurting his feelings. "And I've rescued you, haven't I? Did you ever read about the Knights of the Round Table, and how they rescued ladies in distress? I'm your knight, and you ought to give me a knot of ribbon. They always do in the books."

Zara looked puzzled.

"Haven't you ever read about them?" said Jack, looking disappointed. But then he turned to Bessie. "You have, haven't you?"

"I certainly have, Jack, and Zara shall, soon. They were brave men, Zara, who lived centuries ago. And whenever they saw a lady who needed help they gave it to her. Jack's quite right; he is like them."

Jack flushed with pleasure. He had liked Bessie from the start and now he adored her.

"You're Zara's true knight, Jack, and she'll give you that ribbon from her hair. But you mustn't let anyone see it, or tell about this adventure, unless your father asks you. You mustn't say anything that isn't true, but only answer questions. Don't offer to tell people, or else you may be punished, because Farmer Weeks would say we were bad, and that it was wrong to help us."

"I wouldn't believe him, and neither would my pop, I know that. He's the greatest man that ever lived—greater than George Washington. And he'll say I was just right if I tell him. I just know he will."

"But maybe he and Farmer Weeks are friends, Jack. Then he'd think it was all wrong, wouldn't he?"

"My pop wouldn't have him for a friend, Bessie, don't you believe he would! My pop would never lock a girl up in a room by herself without her dinner, even if she'd been bad."

"I wonder why they're so long coming back," said Bessie, finally. "Won't they miss you, Jack?"

"Not if I get back in time for supper. They don't care what I do when it's a holiday, like this. They know I know my way around here, and there aren't any wild animals. I wish there were!"

"Wouldn't you be afraid of them?"

"Not a bit of it! I'd have a gun, and I'd shoot them, just as quick as quick!"

"Even if they weren't trying to hurt you?"

"Yes, why shouldn't I? Everyone does, in all the books."

"But we don't act the way people in books do, Jack. We can't. Things aren't just that way. Books are to read, to learn things, and for fun, but we've got to remember that real life's different."

"Well, I bet if I saw a lion coming through that wood there I'd kill him."

"Suppose he ate you up first?" asked Zara.

"He'd better not! My pop'd catch and make him sorry he ever did anything like that! Say, it is taking them a long time to come back. Maybe they've lost their way."

"Could they around here?"

"You bet they could! Lots of people do, from the hotel, and we have to send out and find them, so's they don't have to stay out all night. Say, did you hear something just then?"

They listened attentively, and presently Zara keen ears detected a sound.

"There's someone coming," she said. "Listen! You can hear them quite plainly now."

They were quiet for a minute.

"They must be quite close," said Zara, then. "We heard them much further off than that when they were coming after us. I wonder why they got so near before we heard them this time?"

"That's easily explained, Zara," said Bessie. "When they were going the wind was behind them. Now it's in front of them. And they were going up hill, too, so there may have been an echo, because they were shouting toward the rocks upon the hill. Now that's changed, too."

"Say, you're a regular scout!" said Jack approvingly. "I knew all that, but I didn't suppose girls knew things like that. Say, when I get old enough I'm going to be a Boy Scout. That'll be fine, won't it? I'll have a uniform, and a badge, and everything."

"Splendid, Jack! We're going to be Camp Fire Girls, and we'll have rings, and badges, too."

"What are Camp Fire Girls? Are they like the Boy Scouts?"

"Something like them, Jack. Sometime, when I know more about them, I'll come back and tell you all about it. I know it's nice—but I don't really know much more than that yet."

Then they had to be still again, for the voices of the returning hunters were very plain. They could hear Farmer Weeks, loud and angry, in the lead.

"Ain't it the beatin'est thing you ever heard of?" he was asking one of his companions. "How do you guess that little varmint ever got away?"

"Better give it up as a bad job, old hayseed," said another voice. "She's too slick for you—and I can't say I'm sorry, either. Way you've been goin' on here makes me think anyone'd be glad to dig out and run away from a chance to work for you."

"Any lazy good-for-nothing like you would—yes," said Farmer Weeks, enraged by the taunt. "I make anyone that gits my pay or my vittles work—an' why shouldn't they? If you'd gone on, like I wanted you to, we'd have caught her."

"We ain't workin' for you, an' we never will, neither," said the other man, laughing. "Better be careful how you start callin' us names, I can tell you. If you ain't you may go home with a few of them whiskers of your'n pulled out."

"You shut your trap!"

"Sure! I'd rather hear you talk, anyhow. You're so elegant and refined like. Makes me sorry I never went to collidge, so's I could talk that way, too."

They couldn't make out what Farmer Weeks replied to that. He was so angry that he just mumbled his words, and didn't get them out properly. Zara was smiling, her eyes shining. But then the old farmer's voice rose loud and clear again, just as he passed the cave.

"I'll git her yet," he said, vindictively. "I know what she's done, all right. She's gone traipsin' off with that passel of gals that Paw Hoover sold his garden truck to yesterday. I heard 'em laughin' and chatterin' back there on the road where I found her. She'll go runnin' back to 'em—and I'll show 'em, I will!"

"Aw, you're all talk and no do," said the other man, contemptuously. "You talk big, but you don't do a thing."

"I'll have the law on 'em. That gal's as good as mine for the time till she's twenty-one, an' I'll show 'em whether they can run off that way with a man's property. Guess even a farmer's got some rights—an' I can afford to pay for lawin' when I need it done."

"I s'pose you can afford to pay us for runnin' off on this wild goose chase for you, then? Hey?"

"Not a cent—not a cent!" they heard Farmer Weeks say, angrily. "I ain't a-goin' to give none of my good money that I worked for to any low-down shirkers like you—hey, what are you doin' there, tryin' to trip me up?"

A chorus of laughter greeted his indignant question, but he seemed to take the hint, for the fugitives in the cave heard no more talk from him, although for some time after that the sounds in the direction the pursuers had taken on their return to the inn were plain enough.

When the last sounds had died away, and they were quite sure that they were safe, for the time, at least, Bessie got up.

"Suppose we follow this trail right up the way they went?" Bessie asked Jack. "Where will it bring us?"

"To the top of the mountain," said Jack. "But if you want to go off that way I'll walk a way with you, and show you where you can strike off and come to another trail that will bring you out on the main road to Zebulon."

"That'll be fine, Jack. If you'll do that, you'll help us ever so much, and we'll be able to get along splendidly."

"We'd better start," said Zara, nervously. "I want to get away as soon as ever I can. Don't you, Bessie?"

"Indeed I do, Zara. I'm just as afraid of having Farmer Weeks catch us as you are. If he found me he'd take me back to Maw Hoover, I know. And she'd be awfully angry with me."

"I'm all ready to start whenever you are," announced Jack. "Come on. It gets dark early in the woods, you know. They're mighty thick when you get further up the mountain. But if you walk along fast you'll get out of them long before it's really dark."

So they started off. Little Jack seemed to be a thorough woodsman and to know almost every stick and stone in the path. And presently they came to a blazed tree—a tree from which a strip of bark had been cut with a blow from an axe.

"That's my mark. I made it myself," said Jack, proudly. "Here's where we leave this trail. Be careful now. Look where I put my feet, and come this same way."

Then he struck off the trail, and into the deep woods themselves where the moss and the carpet of dead leaves deadened their footsteps. Although the sun was still high, the trees were so thick that the light that came down to them was that of twilight, and Zara shuddered.

"I'd hate to be lost in these woods," she said.

Then, abruptly, they were on another trail. Jack had been a true guide.

"You can't lose your way now," he said. "Keep to the trail and go straight ahead."

"Good-bye, Jack," said Bessie. "You're just as true and brave as any of the knights you ever read about, and if you keep on like this you'll be a great man when you grow up—as great as your father. Good-bye!"

"Good-bye and thank you ever so much," called Zara.

"Come again!" said Jack, and stood there until they were out of sight.

It was not long before they came out near the main road, and now Zara gave a joyful cry.

"Oh, I'm so glad to be here!" she exclaimed. "Those woods frightened me, Bessie. They were so dark and gloomy. And it's so good to see the sun again, and the fields and the blue sky!"

Bessie looked about her curiously as she strove to get her bearings. Then her face cleared.

"I know where we are now," she said. "We're still quite a little distance from where we stopped for lunch and Farmer Weeks got hold of you, Zara. We'll have to go up the road. You see, it brought us quite a little out of our direct way—going back in the woods as we did. But it was worth it—to get away from Farmer Weeks."

"I should think it was!" said Zara. "I'd walk on my hands for a mile to be free from him. He was awful. He drove up just as I got down to the road, and as soon as I saw him I started to run. But I was so frightened that my knees shook, and he jumped out and caught me."

"What did he say to you?"

"Oh, everything! He said he could have me put in prison for running away, and he asked me where you were, but I wouldn't say a thing. I wouldn't even answer him when he asked me if I'd seen you. And he said that when I came to work for him, he'd see that I got over my laziness and my notions."

"Well, you're free of him now, Zara. Oh!"

"What is it, Bessie?"

"Zara, don't you remember what he said? That he'd find us through the Camp Fire Girls? He knows about them! If we go right back to them now, we may be walking right into his arms. Oh, how I wish I could get hold of Miss Eleanor—of Wanaka!"

They stared at one another in consternation.

CHAPTER IX

A CLOSE SHAVE

"I never thought of that, Bessie! Do you suppose he'd really go after the girls and look for us there?"

"You could hear how mad he was, Zara. I think he'd do anything he could to get even with you for running away like that. It made him look foolish before all those men and it'll be a long time before folks let him forget how he was fooled by a girl."

"What are we going to do?"

"I'm trying to think. If I could get word to Miss Eleanor, she'd know what to tell us, I'm sure. I'm afraid she'll be wondering what's become of me—and maybe she'll think I just ran away, and think I was wrong to do it."

"But she'll understand when you tell her about it, Bessie, and if you hadn't come I never would have got away by myself. I'd have been afraid even to try, if there'd been a chance."

"The worst part of it is that if Farmer Weeks really has any right to keep you, or if you were wrong to run away, it might get Miss Eleanor into trouble if they could find out that she's been helping you to get away."

They were walking along the road, but now Bessie, who had forgotten the need of caution in her consternation at the thought of the new plight they faced, pulled Zara after her into the bushes beside the highway.

"I heard wheels behind us," she explained. "We mustn't take any chances."

They stopped to let the wagon they had heard pass by, but as it came along Bessie cried out suddenly.

"That's Paw Hoover!" she said. "And I'm going to speak to him, and ask him what he thinks we ought to do. I'm sure he'll give us good advice, and that he's friendly to us."

She hailed him, and the old farmer, mightily surprised at the sound of her voice, pulled up his horses.

"Whoa!" he shouted. "Well, Bessie! Turning up again like a bad penny. What's the matter now?"

Breathlessly Bessie told him what had happened, and of Zara's escape from Farmer Weeks, while Zara interrupted constantly to supply some detail her chum had forgotten.

"Well, by gravy, I dunno what to say!" said Paw Hoover, scratching his head and looking at them with puzzled eyes. "I don't like Silas Weeks—never did!

I'd hate to have a girl of mine bound over to him—that I would! But these lawyers beat me! I ain't never had no truck with them."

"Will the law make Zara go to him, Paw?" asked Bessie.

"I dunno, Bessie—I declare I dunno!" he answered, slowly. "He seems almighty anxious to get hold of her—an' I declare I dunno why. Seems like there must be lots of other girls over there at the poor-farm he could take if he's so powerful anxious, all of a sudden, to have a girl to work for him. I did hear say, though, that he'd got some sort of a paper signed by the judge—an' if that's so, there ain't no tellin' what he can do. Made him her gardeen, I guess, whatever that is."

"But Zara doesn't need a guardian! She's got her father," said Bessie.

Paw shook his head. He looked as if he didn't think much of the sort of guardianship Zara's father would give her. He was a good, just man, but he shared the Hedgeville prejudice against the foreigner.

"I reckon you're right about not wantin' to get those young ladies I saw you with mixed up with Silas, Bessie," he went on, reflectively. "Too bad you can't get hold of that Miss Mercer. She's as bright as a button, she is. Now, if she were here, she'd find a way out of this hole before you could say Jack Robinson!"

"I believe she could, too," said Bessie. "If you'd seen the way she started out after Farmer Weeks when I told her I thought he must have gone to Zebulon!"

"Zebulon? Was she a goin' there? Then maybe she ain't come back yet, an' we could meet her on the way. Eh?"

"Oh, I'm afraid she must have gone back to the girls long ago," said Bessie.

"Well, you jump in behind there, and get under cover. Ain't no one goin' to look in—you'll be snug there, if it is a mite hot. An' I'll just drive along an' see if I can't meet your Miss Mercer. Then we'll know what to do. An' I'll spell it over, an' maybe I'll hit on some way to help you out myself, even if we don't meet her. Like as not I'll come across Silas Weeks, too, but he'll never suspicion that you're in here with me. Ha! Ha! Not in a million years, he won't. No, sir!"

Bessie laughed, and she and Zara jumped in happily.

"We've got ever so many friends, after all, Zara," she said, in a whisper, as they drove along. "Look at Paw Hoover. He's been as nice as he can be, and he thinks I set his place on fire, too! I'm sure things will be all right. We'll find the girls again, and everything will be just as we had planned."

"Bessie, why do you suppose Farmer Weeks is so set on having me to work for him? Doesn't that seem funny to you? I'm not as clever as lots of girls he could get, I'm sure."

"I can't guess, Zara. But we'll find out sometime, never fear. Did he and your father ever have anything to do with one another?"

"They did just at first when we came out here. He came over to our place in the evenings a good deal, and he and my father used to talk together. But I never knew what they talked about."

"Did they seem friendly?"

"They were at first."

"Then I should think he would have tried to help your father when there was trouble."

"No, no! They had an awful quarrel one night, and my father said he was as bad as some of the people who hated him in Europe, and that he'd have to look out for him. He said he was so rich that people would do what he wanted, and after that he was afraid, and whenever he did any work, he used to get me to stay around outside the house and tell him if anyone came. And he always used to say that it was Farmer Weeks he wanted me to look out for most."

"Well, there's not much use in our thinking about it, Zara. The more we puzzle our brains over it, the less we'll know about it, I'm afraid."

"That's so, too, Bessie. I'm awfully sleepy. I can hardly keep my eyes open."

"Don't try. You've had a hard time to-day. Get to sleep if you can. I'll wake you up if there's any need for it. I'm tired, but I'm not sleepy at all, and this ride will rest me splendidly."

Bessie peeped out now and then, and she kept her eyes open on the lookout for the spring where Farmer Weeks had surprised Zara. But when they passed it, although she looked out and listened hard, she couldn't tell whether the Camp Fire Girls were on the bluff above the roadside or not, and she was afraid to ask Paw Hoover to stop and let her find out for certain, since there was the chance that Farmer Weeks might have returned with the idea that Zara, having escaped his clutches, would naturally have come back to the place of her capture.

Bessie understood very well that, while Paw Hoover was proving himself a true friend, and was evidently willing to do all he could for them, it would never do for Silas Weeks or anyone else from Hedgeville to know that he was befriending the two fugitives. She could guess what Maw Hoover would say to him if she learned that he had helped her, and if there was the chance that Farmer Weeks might get Miss Mercer into trouble through her friendship for them, Paw Hoover was running the same risk.

Until after they reached the crossroads where Bessie had so fortunately been led to take the right turn in her pursuit of Zara earlier in the day, they did not pass or meet a single vehicle of any sort, nor even anyone on foot. Zara slept soundly, and Bessie, soothed by the motion of the wagon, was beginning to nod sleepily.

She had almost dozed off when she was aroused sharply by a sudden shout to his horses from Paw Hoover, and she heard him call out laughingly:

"Hello, there, Miss Mercer! Didn't expect to see me again so soon, did you? I'll bet I've got the surprise of your life for you."

Then she heard Wanaka's clear voice.

"Oh, Mr. Hoover! You don't mean—"

"Yes, I do—and the pair of them, too," he said.

"Well, really? Oh, I'm so relieved! I've been half wild about poor little Zara. I wasn't so afraid for Bessie—she's better able to care for herself."

How proud Bessie was when she heard that!

"Jump up, Miss Mercer. Then you can talk to Bessie. She's keeping under cover, like the wise young one she is. I'm afraid there's still trouble stirring, Miss Mercer."

"I know there is, Mr. Hoover," Eleanor answered, gravely. And then she looked through to see Bessie, and in a moment they were in one another's arms.

"I've been to Zebulon, and I've found out lots of things," said Eleanor. "Bessie, unless we're very careful that horrid old Mr. Weeks will get hold of Zara again, and the law will help him to keep her. I don't know how you got her away from him; you can tell me that later. But just now I've thought of a way to beat him."

"I knew you would," said Bessie.

"The law is wrong, sometimes, I'm sure," said Eleanor. "And I'm just as sure that this is one of the times. I've seen Mr. Weeks, and no one would trust Zara to him. He'd treat her harshly, I know, and I don't believe it would be easy to get him punished for it—around here, at least."

"You're right there, ma'am," said Paw Hoover. "Silas Weeks has got too many mortgages around here not to be able to have his own way when he's really sot on getting it."

"Now, listen," said Eleanor quickly to Bessie. "I'm going to change all our plans because I'm sure we can do more good than if we stuck to what we meant to do. Mr. Hoover, can you spare the time to drive Bessie and Zara to the road that crosses this about half a mile before you come to Zebulon, and then a little way down that road, too?"

"I'll make the time," said Paw, heartily.

"Then it's going to be easy. I want them to get to the railroad. There are too many people around the station in Zebulon, and there'd almost surely be someone there who knew them. I'm not sure of just where Mr. Weeks is right now. He might even be there himself. So that's too risky—"

"I see what you're driving at," said Paw, suddenly. His face broke into a smile. "There's a station further down the line—a little no-account station, ain't there? I've seen it."

"Yes, Perryville. But the down train stops there, and it isn't just a flag stop, either. Now, listen, Bessie. Mr. Hoover will take you there, or nearly there, so that you can easily walk the rest of the way. And when you get there don't get by the track until you hear the train coming. Stay where no one is likely to see you, and then, when the train whistles, run over and be ready to get on board. And get off at Pine Bridge—Pine Bridge, do you hear? Will you remember that? When you get there, just wait. I'll be there almost as soon as you are."

Paw Hoover burst into a roar of laughter as he listened.

"Bessie said you'd have a way to beat Silas Weeks, and, great Godfrey, you sure have!" he said. "I never thought of that—but you're right. Get her out of the state, and there ain't no way under heaven that Silas can get hold of the girl unless she comes back of her own accord. Court writs don't run beyond state lines, not unless they're in the Federal court. Godfrey, but you're smart all right, young lady!"

"Thank you," said Eleanor, smiling at him in return for the compliment. "You're sure you understand, Bessie? Here's the money for your fare. You won't have time to buy tickets, so just give the money to the conductor."

Then she dropped from the wagon to the road and Paw Hoover whipped up his horses.

"You sleep, if you can, Bessie," he said. "I'll wake you up when it's time to get down."

And Bessie, her mind relieved, was glad to obey. It seemed to her that she had only just gone to sleep when Paw Hoover shook her gently to arouse her.

"Here we are," he said. "Station's just over there—see, beyond the bend. Remember what Miss Mercer told you, now, and good luck, Bessie! I reckon we'll see you again sometime."

There were tears in Bessie's eyes as she said good-bye. She watched him drive off, and then she and Zara sat down to wait for the coming of the train. They sat on the grass, behind a cabin that had been abandoned, where they could see the track while they themselves were hidden from anyone approaching by the road they had come. And before long the rails began to hum. Then, in the distance, there was the shriek of a whistle.

"Come on, Zara," cried Bessie, and they ran toward the station, just as the train came into sight, its brakes grinding as it slowed down.

And then, as they climbed aboard, there was the sudden sound of galloping hoofs, and of hoarse shouting. Farmer Weeks, in his buggy, raced toward the train, his hands lifted as he called wildly to the conductor to stop.

CHAPTER X

OUT OF THE WOODS

The train only stopped for a moment at the little station. Seldom, indeed, did it take on any passengers. And on that trip it was already late. Even as the two girls climbed up the steps the brakeman gave his signal, the conductor flung out his hand, and the wheels began to move. And Farmer Weeks, jumping out of his buggy, raced after it, yelling, but in vain.

Swiftly the heavy cars gathered speed. And Bessie and Zara, frightened by their narrow escape, were still too delighted by the way in which Farmer Weeks had been baffled to worry. They felt that they were safe now.

"I suppose that old hick thought we'd stop the train for him," they heard the conductor say to the brakeman. "Well, he had another guess coming! Look at him, will you?"

"He's mad all through!" said the brakeman, laughing, "Well, he had a right to be there when the train got in. If we waited for every farmer that gets to the station late, we'd be laid off in a hurry, I'll bet."

Bessie and Zara were in the last car of the train, and they could look back as it sped away.

"See, Zara, he's standing there, waving his arms and shaking his fist at us," she said.

"He can't hurt us that way, Bessie. Well, all I hope is that we've seen the last of him. Is it true that he can't touch me except in this state?"

"That's what Wanaka said, Zara. And she must know."

Then the conductor came around.

"We didn't get our tickets, so here's the money," said Bessie. "We want to get to Pine Bridge."

"You didn't have much more time than you needed to catch this train," said the conductor, as he took the money. "Pine Bridge, eh? That's our first stop. You can't make any mistake."

"How soon do we cross the state line, Mr. Conductor?" asked Zara, anxiously.

The conductor looked out of the window.

"Right now," he said. "See that white house there? Well, that's almost on the line. The house is in one state, and the stable's in the other. Why are you so interested in that?" He looked at them in sudden suspicion. "Here, was that your father who was so wild because he didn't catch the train? Were you running away from him?"

Bessie's heart sank. She wondered if the conductor, should be really be suspicious, could make them go back, or keep them from getting off the train at Pine Bridge.

"No, he wasn't any relative of ours at all," she said.

"Seems to me he was shouting about you two, though," said the conductor. "Hey, Jim!"

He called the brakeman.

"Say, Jim, didn't it look to you like that hayseed was trying to stop these two from gettin' aboard instead of tryin' to catch the train himself?"

"Never thought of that," said Jim, scratching his head. "Guess maybe he was, though. Maybe we'd better send 'em back from Pine Bridge."

"That's what I'm thinking," said the conductor.

"We've paid our fare. You haven't any right to do that," said Bessie, stoutly, although she was frightened. "And I tell you that man isn't our father. He hasn't got anything to do with us—"

"He seemed to think so, and I believe that was why you came running that way to catch the train, without any tickets. You say he's not your father. Who is he? Do you know him at all?"

Bessie wished she could say that she did not; wished she could, truthfully, deny knowing Farmer Weeks at all. But not even to avert what looked like a serious danger would she lie.

"Yes, we know him," she said. "He's a farmer from Hedgeville. And—"

"Hedgeville, eh? What's his name?"

"Weeks—Silas Weeks."

The effect of the name was extraordinary. Conductor and brakeman doubled up with laughter, and for a moment, while the two girls stared, neither of them could speak at all. Then the conductor found his voice.

"Oh, ho-ho," he said, still laughing. "I wouldn't have missed that for a week's pay! If I could only have seen his face! Don't you worry any more! We'll not send you back to him, even if you were running from him. Don't blame anyone for tryin' to get away from that old miser!"

"Wish he'd tried to jump aboard after we started," said Jim, the brakeman. "I'd have kicked him off, and I wouldn't have done it gently, either!"

"We know Silas Weeks," explained the conductor. "He's the worst kicker and trouble maker that ever rode on this division. Every time he's aboard my train he gives us more trouble in one trip than all the other passengers give us in ten. He's always trying to beat his way without payin' fare, and scarcely a time goes by that he don't write to the office about Jim or me."

"Lot of good that does him," said Jim. "They don't pay any attention to him."

"No, not now. They're getting used to him, and they know what sort of a mischief maker he is. But he's a big shipper, an' at first they used to get after me pretty hard when he wrote one of his kicks."

"Before I came on the run, you mean?"

"Sure! He'd been at it a long time before I got you, Jim. You see, he sends so much stuff by freight they had to humor him—and they still do. But now they just write him a letter apologizin' and don't bother me about it at all. Bet I've lost as much as a week's pay, I guess, goin' to headquarters in workin' time to explain his kicks. He's got a swell chance of gettin' help from me!"

Then the two trainmen passed on, but not until they had promised to see the two girls safe off the car at Pine Bridge.

"People usually get paid back when they do something mean, Zara," said Bessie. "If Farmer Weeks hadn't treated those men badly, they would probably have sent us back. But as soon as they heard who he was, you saw how they acted."

"That's right, Bessie. I bet he'd be madder than ever if he knew that. Someone ought to tell him."

"He'd only try to make more trouble for them, and perhaps he could, too. No, I don't want to bother about him any more, Zara. I just want to forget all about him. I wonder how long we'll have to wait at Pine Bridge."

"Miss Eleanor didn't say what she was going to do, did she?"

"No; she just said that she'd get there, and that she had decided to change all her plans on our account."

"We're making an awful lot of trouble for her, Bessie."

"I know we are, and we've got to show her that we're grateful and do anything we can to help her, if she ever needs our help. I thought when we started from Hedgeville after the fire that we would be able to get along together somehow, Zara, but I see now how foolish that was."

"I believe you'd have managed somehow, Bessie. You can do 'most anything, I believe."

"I'm afraid you'll find out that I can't before we're done, Zara. We didn't have any money, or any plans, or anything. It certainly was lucky for us that we went to that lake where the Camp Fire Girls were. If it hadn't been for them we'd be back in Hedgeville now, and much worse off than if we hadn't tried to get away."

"There's the whistle, Bessie. I guess that means we're getting near Pine Bridge."

"Well, here you are! Going to meet your friends here?" said the conductor.

"Yes; thank you," said Bessie. "We're ever so much obliged, and we'll be all right now."

"You sit right down there on that bench in front of the station," advised the conductor. "Don't move away, or you'll get lost. Pine Bridge is quite a place. Bigger than Hedgeville—quite a bit bigger. And if anyone tries to bother you, just you run around to the street in front of the station, and you'll find a fat policeman there. He's a friend of mine, and he'll look after you if you tell him Tom Norris sent you. Remember my name—Tom Norris."

"Thank you, and good-bye, Mr. Norris," they called to him together, as they stepped off the car. Then the whistle blew again, and the train was off.

Although there were a good many people around, no one seemed to pay much attention to the two girls. Everyone seemed busy, and to be so occupied with his own affairs that he had no time to look at strangers or think about what they were doing.

"We're a long way from home now, Zara, you see," said Bessie. "I guess no one here will know us, and we'll just wait till Miss Eleanor comes."

"Maybe she's here already, waiting for us."

"Oh, I don't think so."

"We'd better look around, though. How is she going to get here, Bessie?"

"I don't know. She never told me about that. We were talking as fast as we could because we were afraid Farmer Weeks might come along any time, and that would have meant a lot of trouble."

"Suppose he follows us here, Bessie?"

"He won't! He'll know that we're safe from him as soon as we're out of the state. I'm not afraid of him now—not a bit, and you needn't be, either."

"Well, if you're not, I'll try not to be. But I wish Miss Eleanor would come along, Bessie. I'll feel safer then, really."

"You've been brave enough so far, Zara. You mustn't get nervous now that we're out of the woods. That would be foolish."

"I suppose so, but I wasn't really brave before, Bessie. I was terribly frightened when he locked me in that room. I didn't see how anyone would know what had become of me, or how they could find out where I was in time to help me."

"Did you think about trying to run away by yourself?"

"Yes, indeed, but I was afraid I'd get lost. I didn't know where we were. I'd never been that way before."

"It's a good thing you waited, Zara. Even if you had got away and got into those woods where Jack took us, it would have been dangerous. You might easily have got lost, and it's the hardest thing to find people who are in the woods."

"Why?"

"Because they get to wandering around in circles. If you can see the sun, you can know which way you're going, and you can be sure of getting somewhere, if you only keep on long enough. But in the woods, unless you know a lot of things, there's nothing to guide you, and people just seem, somehow, bound to walk in a circle. They keep on coming back to the place they started from."

Pine Bridge was a junction point, and while the girls waited, patiently enough, it began to grow dark. Several trains came in, but, though they looked anxiously at the passengers who descended from each one of them, there was no sign of Miss Mercer.

"I hope nothing's happened to her," said Zara anxiously.

"Oh, we mustn't worry, Zara. She's all right, and she'll come along presently."

"But suppose she didn't, what should we do?"

"We'd be able to find a place to spend the night. I've got money, you know, and the policeman would tell us where to go, if we went to him, as the conductor told us to do."

Another train came in on the same track as the one that had brought them. Again they scanned its passengers anxiously, but no one who looked at all like Miss Mercer got off, and they both sighed as they leaned back against the hard bench. Neither of them had paid any attention to the other passengers, and they were both startled and dismayed when a tall, gaunt figure loomed up suddenly before them, and they heard the harsh voice of Farmer Weeks, chuckling sardonically as he looked down on them.

"Caught ye, ain't I?" he said. "You've given me quite a chase—but I've run you down now. Come on, you Zara!"

He seized her hand, but Bessie snatched it from him.

"You let her alone!" she said, with spirit. "You've no right to touch her!"

"I'll show you whether I've any right or not, and I'm going to take her back with me!" Farmer Weeks said, furiously. "Come on, you baggage! You'll not make a fool of me again, I'll promise you that!"

"Come on," said Bessie, suddenly. She still held Zara's hand, and before the surprised farmer could stop them, Bessie had dragged Zara to her feet, and they had dashed under his outstretched arm and got clear away, while the loafers about the station laughed at him.

"Come back! You can't get away!" he shouted, as he broke into a clumsy run after them. "Come back, or I'll make you sorry—"

But Bessie knew what she was about. Without paying the slightest attention to his angry cries, she ran straight around to the front of the station, and there she found the fat policeman.

"Won't you help us?" she cried. "Mr. Norris, the conductor, said you would—"

"What's wrong?" said the policeman, starting. He had been dozing. "Any friend of Tom's is a friend of mine—here, here, none of that!"

The last remark was addressed to Farmer Weeks, who had come up and seized Zara.

"I've got an order saying I've a right to take her," exclaimed Weeks.

"But it's not good in this state—" interrupted Bessie.

"Let's see it," said the policeman.

Weeks, storming and protesting, showed him the court order.

"That's no good here. You'll have to get her into the state where it was issued before you can use that," said the policeman.

"You're a liar! I'll take her now—"

The policeman's club was out, and he threatened Weeks with it.

"You touch her and I'll run you in," he said, angrily. "We don't stand for men laying their hands on girls and women in this town. Get away with you now! If I catch you hanging around here five minutes from now, I'll take you to the lock-up, and you can spend the night in a cell."

"But—" began Weeks.

"Not a word more—or I'll do as I say," said the policeman. He was energetic, if he was fat, and he had put a protective arm about Zara. Weeks looked at him and then he slunk off.

And, as he went, the girls heard a merry chorus, "Wo-he-lo, Wo-he-lo," just as another train puffed in.

CHAPTER XI

THE CALL OF THE FIRE

"Wo-he-lo!"

How they did thrill at the sound of the watchword of the Camp Fire! How clearly, now, they understood the meaning of the three syllables, that had seemed to them so mysterious, so utterly without meaning, when they had first heard them on the shores of the lake, as, surprised, they peeped out and saw the merry band of girls who had awakened them after their flight from Hedgeville.

For a moment, so overjoyed were they, they couldn't move at all. But then the spell was broken, as the call sounded again, loud and clear, rising above the noises of the engine that was puffing and snorting on the other side of the station. Farmer Weeks, a black look in his eyes as he shot them a parting glance full of malice, was forgotten as he slunk off.

"Thank you, oh, thank you!" cried Bessie to the astonished policeman, who looked as if he were about to begin asking them questions. "Come on, Zara!"

And, hand in hand, they raced around to the other side of the station again, but blithely, happily this time, and not in terror of their enemy, as they had come. And there, looking about her in all directions, was Eleanor Mercer, and behind her all the girls of the Manasquan Camp Fire.

"Oh, I'm so glad! I was afraid something had happened to you!" cried Eleanor. "But now it's all right! We're all here, and safe. In this state no one can hurt you—either of you!"

Laughing and full of questions, the other girls crowded around Zara and Bessie, so happily restored to them.

"We feel as if you were real Camp Fire Girls already!" said Eleanor Mercer, half crying with happiness. "The girls were wild with anxiety when they found you had gone away, too, Bessie, even though we hadn't told them everything. But they were delighted when I got back and told them you were safe."

"We were, indeed," said Minnehaha. "But it was awful, Bessie, not to know what had become of you, or how to help you! We'd have done anything we could, but we didn't know a single thing to do. So we had just to wait, and that's the hardest thing there is, when someone you love is in trouble."

Bessie almost broke down at that. Until this wonderful meeting with the Camp Fire Girls no one but Zara had loved her, and the idea that these girls really did love her as they said—and had so nobly proved—was almost too much for her. She tried to say so.

"Of course we love one another," said Eleanor. "That's one of the laws of the Fire, and it's one of the words we use to make up Wo-he-lo, too. So you see that it's just as important as it can be, Bessie."

"Yes, indeed, I do see that. I'd be awfully stupid if I didn't, after the splendid way you've helped us, Miss Eleanor. What are we going to do now?"

"We're going to join the big camp not far from here. Three or four Camp Fires are there together, and Mrs. Chester, who is Chief Guardian in the city, wants us to join them. I talked to her about you two over the long-distance telephone before we got on the train, and she's so anxious to see you, and help me to decide what is best for you to do. You'll love her, Bessie; you're sure to. She's so good and sweet to everyone. All the girls just worship her."

"If she's half as nice as you, we're sure to love her," said Zara.

Eleanor laughed.

"I'm not half as wonderful as you think I am, Zara. But I'm nicer than I used to be, I think."

"Oh!"

"Yes, indeed! I used to be selfish and thoughtless, caring only about having a good time myself, and never thinking about other people at all. But Mrs. Chester talked to me."

"I'll bet she never had a chance to scold you."

"I'm afraid she did, Zara; but she didn't want to. That's not her way. She never scolds people. She just talks to them in that wonderful, quiet way of hers, and makes them see that they haven't been doing right."

"But I don't believe you ever did anything that wasn't right."

"Maybe I didn't mean to, and maybe it wasn't what I did that was wrong. It was more what I didn't do."

"I don't see what you mean."

"Well, I was careless and thoughtless, just as I said. I used to dance, and play games, and go to parties all the time."

"I think that must be fine! Didn't you have to work at home, though?"

"No; and that was just the trouble, you see. My people had plenty of money, and they just wanted me to have a good time. And I did—but I've had a better one since I started doing things for other people."

"I bet you always did, really—"

"I'm not an angel now, Zara, and I certainly never used to be, nor a bit like one. Just because I've happened to be able to help you two a little, you think altogether too much of me."

"Oh, no; we couldn't—"

"Well, as I was saying, Mrs. Chester saw how things were going, and she started to talk to me. I was horrid to her at first, and wouldn't pay any attention to her at all."

"I'm going to ask her about that. I don't believe you ever were horrid to anyone."

"Probably Mrs. Chester won't admit it, but it's true, just the same, Bessie. But she talked to me, and kept on talking, and she made me think about all the poorer girls who had to work so hard and couldn't go to parties. And I began to feel sorry, and wonder what I could do to make them happier."

"You see, that's just what we said! You weren't selfish at all!"

"I tried to stop as soon as I found out that I had been, Zara; that's all. And I think anyone would do that. It's because people don't think of the unhappiness and misery of others that there's so much suffering, not because they really want other people to be unhappy."

"I guess that's so. I suppose even Farmer Weeks wouldn't be mean if he really thought about it."

"I'm sure he wouldn't—and we'll have to try to reform him, too, before we're done with him. You see, if there were more people like Mrs. Chester, things would be ever so much nicer. She heard about the Camp Fire Girls, and she saw right away that it meant a chance to make things better, right in our home town."

"Is that how it all started?"

"Yes, with us. And it was the same way all over the country, because, really, there are lots and lots of noble, unselfish women like Mrs. Chester, who want everyone to be happy."

"Is she as pretty as you, Miss Eleanor?"

"Much prettier, Zara; but you won't think about that after you've talked to her. She got hold of me and some of the other girls like me, who had lots of time and money, and she made us see that we'd be twice as happy if we spent some of our time doing things for other people, instead of thinking about ourselves the whole time. And she's been perfectly right."

"I knew you enjoyed doing things like that—"

"Yes; so you see it isn't altogether unselfish, after all. But Mrs. Chester says that we ought all try to be happy ourselves, because that's the best way to make other people happy, after all, as long as we never forget that there are others, and that we ought to think of serving them."

"That's like in the Bible where it says, 'It is more blessed to give than to receive,' isn't it?"

"That's the very idea, Bessie! I'm glad you thought of that yourself. That's just the lesson we've all got to learn."

"But we haven't been able to help anyone yet, Miss Eleanor. Everyone's helping us—"

"Don't you worry about that, Bessie. You'll have lots of chances to help others—ever so many! Just you wait until you get to the city. There are lots of girls there who are more wretched than you—girls who don't get enough to eat, and have to work so hard that they never have any fun at all, because when they get through with their work they're so tired they have to go right to sleep."

"Bessie was like that, Miss Eleanor."

"I'm afraid she was, Zara. But we're going to change all that. Mrs. Chester has promised to help, and that means that everything will be all right."

"Do you think I could ever do anything to help anyone else, Miss Eleanor?"

"I'm sure you have already, Zara. You've been a good friend to Bessie, and I know you've cheered her up and helped her to get through days when she was feeling pretty bad."

"Indeed she has, Miss Eleanor! Many and many a time! Since I've known her I've often wondered how I ever got along at all before she came to Hedgeville!"

"You see, Zara, doing things for others doesn't mean always that you're spending money or actually doing something. Sometimes the very best help you can give is by just being cheerful and friendly."

"I hadn't thought of that. But I'm going to try always to be like that. Miss Eleanor, when can we be real Camp Fire Girls?"

"I talked to Mrs. Chester about that to-day, and I think it will be to-night, Bessie."

"Oh, that will be splendid!"

"Yes, won't it? You see, it's the night for our Council Fire—that's when we take in new members, and award honors and report what we've done. We hold one every moon. That's the Indian name for month. You see, month just means moon, really. This is the Thunder Moon of the Indians, the great copper red moon. It's our month of July."

"And will we learn to sing the songs like the other girls?"

"Yes, indeed. You'll find them very easy. They're very beautiful songs and I think we're very lucky to have them."

"Who wrote them? Girls that belong?"

"Some of them, but not all, or nearly all. We have found many beautiful songs about fire and the things we love that were written by other poets who never heard of the Camp Fire Girls at all. And yet they seem to be just the right songs for us."

"That's funny, isn't it, Miss Eleanor?"

"Not a bit, Zara. Because the Camp Fire isn't a new thing, really. Not the big idea that's back of it, that you'll learn as you stay with us, and get to know more about us. All we hope to do is to make our girls fine, strong women when they get older, like all the great brave women that we read about in history. They've all been women who loved the home, and all it means—and the fire is the great symbol of the home. It was fire that made it possible for people to have real homes."

"I've read lots and lots of things about fire," said Bessie. "Longfellow, and Tennyson, and other poets."

But then her face darkened suddenly.

"It was fire that got me into trouble, though," she said. "The fire that Jake Hoover used to set the woodshed afire."

"That was because he was misusing the fire, Bessie. Fire is a great servant. It's the most wonderful thing man ever did—learning to make a fire, and tend it, and control it. Have you heard what it says in the Fire-Maker's Desire? But, of course, you haven't. You haven't been at a Council Fire yet. Listen:

"For I will tend,

As my fathers have tended

And my father's fathers

Since Time began

The Fire that is called

The love of man for man—

The love of man for God."

"That's a great promise, you see, Bessie. It's a great honor to be a Fire-Maker."

"I see, Miss Eleanor. Yes, it must be. How does one get to be a Fire-Maker? One begins by being a Wood-Gatherer, doesn't one?"

"Yes, and all one has to do to be a Wood-Gatherer is to want to obey the law of the Fire—the seven points of the law. I'll teach you that Desire before the Council Fire to-night. To be a Fire-Maker you have to serve faithfully as a Wood-Gatherer, and you have to do a lot of things that aren't very easy—though they're not very hard, either."

"And you talked about awarding honors. What are they?"

"Have you seen the necklaces the girls wear?"

"Oh, yes! They're beautiful. They look like the ones I've seen in pictures of Indians. But I never thought they were so pretty before, because I've only seen pictures, and they didn't show the different colors of the beads."

"That's just it, Bessie. Those beads are given for honors, and when a girl has enough of them they make the necklaces. They're awarded for all sorts of things—for knowing them, and for doing them, too. And you'll learn to tell by the colors of the beads just what sort of honors they are—why the girl who wears them got them, and what she did to earn them."

"I'm going to work awfully hard to get honors," said Zara, impulsively. "Then, when I can wear the beads, everyone will know about it, and about how I worked to get them. Won't they, Miss Eleanor?"

"Yes, but you mustn't think about it just that way, Zara. You won't, either, when you've earned them. You'll know then that the pleasure of working for the honors is much greater than being able to wear the beads."

"I know why—because it means something!"

"That's just it, Bessie. I can see that you're going to be just the sort of girl I want in my Camp Fire. Anyone who had the money—and they don't cost much—could buy the beads and string them together. But it's only a Camp Fire Girl, who's worked for honors herself, who knows what it really means, and sees that the beads are just the symbol of something much better."

"Aren't there Torch-Bearers, too, Miss Eleanor?"

"Yes. That's the highest rank of all. We haven't any Torch-Bearer in our Camp Fire yet, but we will have soon, because when you girls join us there'll be nineteen girls, and there ought to be a Torch-Bearer."

"She'd help you, wouldn't she, Miss Eleanor?"

"Yes, she'd act as Guardian if I were away, and she'd be my assistant. This is her desire, you know, 'That light which has been given to me, I desire to pass undimmed to others.'"

"I'm going to try to be a Torch-Bearer whenever I can," said Zara.

"There's no reason why you shouldn't be, Zara. That ought to be the ambition of every Camp Fire Girl—to be able, sometime, to help others to get as much good from the Camp Fire as she has herself."

While they talked it had been growing darker. And now Miss Mercer called to the girls.

"We're going to be driven over to the big camp, girls," she said. "I think we've had quite enough tramping for one day. I don't want you to be so tired that you won't enjoy the Council Fire to-night."

There was a chorus of laughter at that, as if the idea that they could ever be too tired to enjoy a Council Fire was a great joke—as, indeed, it was.

But, just the same, the idea of a ride wasn't a bit unwelcome. The troubles of Bessie and Zara had caused a sudden change in the plans of the Camp Fire, as Miss Mercer had made them originally, and they had had a long and strenuous day. So they greeted the big farm wagons that presently rolled up with a chorus of laughs and cheers, and the drivers blinked with astonishment as they heard the Wohelo cheer ring out.

There were two of the wagons, so that there was room for all of them without crowding. Bessie and Zara rode in the first one, close to Wanaka, who had, of course, taken them under her wing.

"You stay close by me," she said to them. "I want you to meet Mrs. Chester as soon as we get to the camp."

"Where is it?"

"That's the surprise I told the girls I had for them this morning. A friend of Mrs. Chester, who has a beautiful place near here, has let us use it for a camping ground. It's the most wonderful place you ever saw. There are deer, quite tame, and all sorts of lovely things. But you'll see more of that in the morning, of course. We've all got to be ever so careful, though, not to frighten the deer or to hurt anything about the place. It's very good of General Seeley to let us be there at all, and we must show him that we are grateful. For the girls who couldn't get far away from the city it's been particularly splendid, because they couldn't possibly have such a good time anywhere else that's near by."

"Oh!" cried Bessie, a moment later, as the wagons turned from the road into a lane that was flanked on both sides by great trees. "I never saw a place so pretty!"

Wide lawns stretched all around them. But in the distance a pink glow, among a grove of trees, marked the real home of the Camp Fire.

CHAPTER XII
A NEW SUSPICION

"I think the fire is more beautiful than anything else, almost," said the Guardian, as she looked at it and pointed it out to Bessie and Zara. "It means so much."

"It looks like a welcome, Wanaka."

"That's just what it is—a real, hearty welcome. It shows us that our sisters of the fire are there waiting for us, ready to make us comfortable after the trouble of the day. Around the fire we can forget all the bad things that have happened, and think only of the good."

"It's easy to do that now. I've been frightened since Jake locked Zara up in the woodshed, awfully frightened. And I've been unhappy, too. But I've been happier in these last two days than I ever was before."

"That's the right spirit, Bessie. Make your misfortunes work out so that you think only of the good they bring. That's the way to be happy, always. You know, it's an old, old saying that every cloud has a silver lining, but it's just as true as it's old, too. People laugh at those old proverbs sometimes,—people who think they know more than anyone else ever did—but in the end they usually admit that they don't really know much more about life and happiness than the people who discovered those great truths first, or spoke about them first, even if someone else had discovered them."

"I've been happy, too," said Zara, but there was a break in her voice. "If I only knew that my father was all right, then I wouldn't be able to be anything but happy, now that I know Farmer Weeks can't take me with him."

"You must try not to worry about your father, Zara. I'm sure that all his troubles will be mended soon, just like yours. Don't you feel that someone has been looking after you in all your troubles?"

"Oh, yes! I never, never would have been able to get away from Farmer Weeks except for that—"

"Well, just try to think that He will look after your father, too, Zara. If he has done nothing wrong he can't be punished, you may be sure of that. This isn't Russia, or one of those old countries where people can be sent to prison without having done anything to deserve it, just because other people with more money or more power don't like them. We live in a free country. Be sure that all will turn out right in the end."

"I feel cramped, Miss Eleanor. May I get out and run along by the horses for a little while?"

"Yes, indeed, Zara."

And Wanaka stopped the wagon, so that she could get out.

"Do you want to go, too, Bessie?"

"I think I'd rather ride, Miss Eleanor. I'm awfully tired."

"You shall, then. I want you to do whatever you like to-night. You've certainly done enough to-day to earn the right to rest."

They rode along in silence for a few minutes, while the glow of the great welcoming fire grew brighter.

"Miss Eleanor?"

"Yes, Bessie?"

"Don't you think it's very strange that Farmer Weeks should take so much trouble to try to get hold of Zara?"

"I do, indeed, Bessie. I've been puzzling about that."

"I believe he knows something about her and her father that no one else knows, something that even Zara doesn't know about, I mean. You know, he and Zara's father were very friendly at first—or, at least, they used to see one another a good deal."

"Yes? Bessie, what sort of man is Zara's father? You have seen a good deal of him, haven't you?"

"I used to go to see Zara sometimes, when I was able to get away. And unless he was away on one of his trips he was always around, but he never said much."

"He could speak English, couldn't he?"

"Yes, but not a bit well. And when I first went there he was awfully funny. He seemed to be quite angry because I was there, and as soon as I came, he rushed into one of the rooms, and put a lot of things away, and covered them so I couldn't see them. But Zara talked to him in their own language, and then he was very nice, and he gave me a penny. I didn't want it, but he made me take it and Zara said I ought to have it, too."

"It looks as if he had had something to hide, Bessie. But then a man might easily want to keep people from finding out all about his business without there being anything wrong."

"If you'd seen him, Miss Eleanor, I'm sure you wouldn't think he'd do anything wrong. He had the nicest face, and his eyes were kind. And after that, sometimes, I'd go there when Zara was out, and he was always just as nice and kind as he could be. He used to get me to talk to him, too, so that he could learn to speak English."

"Well, there's something very strange and mysterious about it all. You found this Mr. Weeks there the night he was taken away, didn't you?"

"Yes."

"That looks as if he had something to do with it. I don't know—but we'll find out the truth some time, Bessie."

"I hope it will be soon. And, Miss Eleanor, I've been waiting a long time to find out about myself, too. Sometimes I think I'm worse off than Zara, because I don't know where my father and mother are, or even what became of them."

The Guardian started.

"Poor Bessie!" she said. "But we'll have to try to find out for you. There are ways of doing that that the Hoovers would never think of. And I'm sure there'll be some explanation. They'd never just go away and leave you, without trying to find out if you were well and look after you."

"Not if they could help it, Miss Eleanor." Bessie's eyes filled with tears. "But perhaps they couldn't. Perhaps they are—dead."

"We must try to be cheerful, Bessie. After all, you know, they say no news is good news, and when you don't positively know that something dreadful has happened, you can always go on hoping."

"Oh, I do, Miss Eleanor! Sometimes I've felt so bad that if I hadn't been able to hope, I don't know what I'd have done. And Jake Hoover, he used to laugh at me, and say that I'd never see them again. He said they were just bad people, glad to get rid of me, but I never believed that."

"That's right, Bessie. You keep on hoping, and we'll do all we can to make your hopes true. Hope is a wonderful thing for people who are in trouble. They can always hope that things will be better, and if they only hope hard enough, they will come to believe it. And once you believe a thing, it's half true, especially when it's a question of doing something."

"How do you mean?"

"Why, I'll try to explain. When Mrs. Chester first wanted me to take charge of a Camp Fire, I thought I was just a silly, stupid, useless girl. But she said she knew I wasn't, and that I could make myself useful."

"You certainly have."

"I'm trying, Bessie, all the time. Well, she told me to wish that I might succeed. And I did. And then I began to hope for it and to want it so much that gradually I believed I could. And as soon as I believed it myself, why, it began to come."

"You wanted to so much—that's why, I suppose."

"Yes. You see, when you believe you can do a thing, you don't get discouraged when you fail at first. It's when you're doubtful and think you can't do a thing at all, that it's hardest. Then when anything goes wrong, it's just what you expected, and it makes you surer than ever that you're going to fail."

"Oh, I see that! I understand now, I think."

"Remember that, Bessie. It's done me more good, knowing that, than almost anything else I can think of. When you start to do a thing, no matter how hard it is, be hopeful and confident. Then the set-backs won't bother you, because you'll know that it's just because you've chosen the wrong way, and you go back and start again, looking for the right way."

"Oh, look!" said Bessie, suddenly. "Isn't it growing black? Do you see that big cloud? And I'm sure I felt drops of rain just then."

"I believe it is going to rain. That's too bad. It will spoil the great Council Fire."

"Won't they have it if it rains?"

"I'm not sure whether there's a big enough place inside or not. But, even if there is, it's much better fun to have it out of doors—a great big fire always seems more cheerful if it's under the trees, so that the great shadows can dance about. And the singing sounds so much better in the open air, too. Oh, I do hope this won't be a real storm!"

But that hope was doomed to disappointment. The rain came down slowly at first, and in great drops, but as the wagons neared the fire and got under the shelter of the trees, the wind rose, and soon the rain was pouring down in great sheets, with flashes of lightning now and then. As they climbed out by the fire it hissed and spluttered as the rain fell into it. No girls were in sight.

"They must all have gone in to get out of the rain, or else they'd be out here to welcome us," said the Guardian. "Oh, there's Mrs. Chester! I knew she wouldn't let the rain keep her!"

And Wanaka ran forward to greet a sweet-faced woman whose hair was slightly tinged with grey, but whose face was as rosy and as smiling as that of a young girl. Bessie and Zara followed Eleanor shyly, but Mrs. Chester put them at their ease in a moment.

"I've heard all about you," she said. "And I'm not going to start in by telling you I'm sorry for you, either, because I'm not!"

Had it not been for the laugh that was in her eyes, and her smile, the words might have seemed unkind.

"I don't believe in being sorry for what's past," the Chief Guardian explained at once. "If people are brave and good, trouble only helps them. And it's the future we must think about, always. That is in your own hands now, and I'm sure you're going to deserve to be happy—and if you do, you can't help finding happiness. That's what I mean."

The two girls liked her at once. There was something so motherly, so kind and wholesome about Mrs. Chester, that they felt as if they had known her a long time.

"I don't know about the Council Fire to-night, Eleanor," she said, looking doubtfully at the rain. "It's too damp, I'm afraid, to have it outdoors, and you know that there are so many times when we have to hold the ceremonial fires indoors, that I hate to do it when, by waiting a day, we can have it in this beautiful place."

"Yes, that's so," said Eleanor. "It's almost sure to be clear to-morrow. And in winter, when it gets cold, we can't even hope to be outdoors very much, except for skating and snowshoeing. Do you know, girls, that in winter we sometimes use three candles instead of a real fire?"

"Yes," said Mrs. Chester. "Of course, after all, it's the meaning of the fire, and not just the fire itself that counts. But I think it's better to have both when we can. So I'm afraid you'll have to wait until to-morrow night for your first Council Fire, girls."

Eleanor looked at them. Then she laughed.

"Really, it's a good thing, after all," she said. "They're so tired that they can hardly keep their eyes open now, Mrs. Chester. I hope there's going to be a good, hot supper."

"There certainly is, my dear! And your girls won't have to cook it, either. Just for to-night you're to be guests of honor. And the new Camp Fire—the Snug Harbor camp, you know—begged me so hard to be allowed to cook the meal and serve it, that I agreed. Julia Kent has done wonders with those girls. You'd think they'd been cooking and working all their lives, instead of it having been just the other way 'round. And they simply worship her. Well, there are your tents over there. You'll hear the call to supper in a few minutes."

She turned and left them, and Eleanor led the way to the tents she had pointed out.

"I'm so delighted to hear about the Snug Harbor girls," she told Bessie and Zara. "You know we've wondered how that was going to turn out. There are about a dozen of them, and they're all girls whose parents are rich. They go to Europe, and have motor cars, and lovely clothes, and servants—two or three of them have their own maids, and they've never even learned to keep their own rooms neat."

"But if they're going to cook our supper—"

"That's just it, Bessie. That's what the Camp Fire has done for them. It has taught them that instead of being proud of never having to do anything for themselves, they ought to be ashamed of not knowing how. And before the summer's over I believe they'll be the best of all the Camp Fires in the whole city."

Supper, in spite of the storm that raged outside, was a jolly, happy meal. The girls were tired, but they brightened as the meal was served, and the few mistakes of the amateur waitresses only made everyone laugh.

Taps, the signal for bedtime, sounded early. All the girls, from the different Camp Fires, were together for a moment.

"We'll have the Council Fire to-morrow night," said Mrs. Chester. "And the longer you sleep to-night, the readier you'll be to-morrow for all the things we have to do. Good-night!"

And then, after all the girls together had sung the beautiful "Lay me to sleep in sheltering flame," silence rested on the camp.

Bessie slept like a log. But in the morning she awoke while everyone else was still asleep. In the east the sky was just turning pink, with the first signs of the coming day. The sky was a deep, beautiful blue, and in the west, where it was still dark, the last stars were still twinkling. Bessie sighed with the beauty of everything, and the sense of comfort and peace that she enjoyed. Then she tried to go to sleep again, but she could not. She had too many things to think about. Zara, disturbed by her movements, woke up too, and looked at her sleepily.

"You remember," said Bessie, "that Wanaka told us last night that in a field not far away there were loads and loads of wild strawberries that we could pick? I think I'll get dressed and see if I can't get enough for breakfast, as a surprise."

"Shall I come with you?" asked Zara.

"No," said Bessie, laughing. "You go to sleep again—you're only half awake now!"

She had no trouble in finding the strawberries, although, just because it was so beautiful, she walked around the great estate for quite a while first. It was a wonderful place. Parts of it were beautifully cared for, with smooth, well clipped lawns, and a few old trees; parts were left just as nature had meant them to be, and to Bessie they seemed even more beautiful. And still other acres were turned into farm lands, where there were all sorts of growing crops.

A few gardeners were about, and they smiled at Bessie as they saw her. She saw some of the deer that Eleanor had spoken of, too, who were so tame that they let her come as close as she liked. But she spent little time in looking at them, and when she found the field where the berries grew she had soon picked a great apronful of them. When she returned everyone was up, and she was greeted with cries of joy when the girls saw her burden.

"They'll make our breakfast ever so much nicer," said Eleanor. "It was good of you to think of them."

Not until after breakfast did they see Mrs. Chester—not, indeed, until all the dishes had been washed and put away. And then she approached with a grave face, and called the Guardian aside. They talked together earnestly for a few minutes, and Eleanor's face grew as serious as the Chief Guardian's. Bessie saw that they looked at her more than once as they spoke, and that Eleanor shook her head repeatedly.

"I wonder what can be wrong, Zara," she said. "Do you suppose that Farmer Weeks has been making trouble for us again?"

"Oh, I hope not! Do you think it's about us they're talking?"

"I'm afraid so. See, they're calling me. We'll soon know."

Bessie did indeed, soon know what had happened.

"Bessie," said Mrs. Chester, "did you go anywhere else this morning when you went for berries?"

"I just walked about the place, Mrs. Chester, and looked around. That's all."

"But you were quite alone?"

"Yes, quite alone. I only saw a few men who were working, cutting the grass, and trimming hedges."

"Oh, I'm sorry! Bessie, over there in the woods there's a place that's fenced off, where General Seeley keeps a lot of pheasants. And some time since last night someone has been in there and frightened the mother birds and taken a lot of the eggs. Some of them were broken—and it was not an animal."

Bessie looked frightened and concerned.

"Oh, what a shame! But, Mrs. Chester, you don't think I did it?"

CHAPTER XIII

A TANGLED WEB

Bessie's eyes were full of fear and dismay as she looked at Mrs. Chester and Eleanor. At first she hadn't thought it even possible that they could think she had done anything so cruel as to frighten the birds and steal their eggs, but there was a grave look on their faces that terrified her.

"No, Bessie," said Mrs. Chester, "I don't believe you did—certainly, I don't want to believe anything of the sort."

"I know you didn't do it, Bessie!" cried Eleanor Mercer.

"But General Seeley is very indignant about it, Bessie," Mrs. Chester went on to say. "And some of the men told him that one of the girls from the camp was around very early this morning, before anyone else was up, walking about, and looking at things. So he seemed to think right away that she must have done it. And he sent for me and asked me if I could find out which of you girls had been out."

"Bessie went out openly, and she came back when we were all up," said Eleanor, stoutly. "If she'd been doing anything wrong, Mrs. Chester, she would have tried to get here without being seen, wouldn't she?"

"I know, Eleanor, I know," said Mrs. Chester, kindly. "You think she couldn't have had anything to do with it—and so do I, really. But for Bessie's own sake we want to clear it up, don't we?"

Bessie stood her ground bravely, and kept back the tears, although it hurt her more to have these friends who had been so good to her bothered about her than it would had almost anything happened to her.

"Oh, I wish I'd never seen you, Miss Eleanor!" she cried. "I've done nothing but make trouble for you ever since you found us. I'm so sorry! Zara wanted to come with me this morning, and if I'd let her, she could have told you that I didn't even see the birds."

"It'll all come out right, Bessie," said Mrs. Chester. "I thought perhaps you might have done it by accident, but if you weren't there we'll find out who really did do it, never fear. Now, you had better come with me. General Seeley asked me to bring any of the girls who had been out this morning with me when I went to see him. He will want to talk to you himself, I think."

So Bessie, tears in her eyes, which she tried bravely to keep back, had to go up to the big house that they could see through the trees. It was a big, rambling house, built of grey stone, with many windows, and all about it were beds of flowers. Bessie had never seen a house that was even half so fine.

"General Seeley is very particular about his birds, and all the animals on the place," explained Mrs. Chester, as they made their way toward the house. "Some men keep pheasants just so that they can shoot them in the autumn, and they call that sport. But General Seeley doesn't allow that. He's a kind and gentle man, although he's a soldier."

"Has he ever been in a war, Mrs. Chester?"

"Yes. He's a real patriot, and when his country needed him he went out to fight, like many other brave and gentle men. But, like most men who are really brave, he hates to see anyone or even any animal, hurt. Soldiers aren't rough and brutal just because they sometimes have to go to war and fight. They know so much about how horrible war is that they're really the best friends of peace."

"I never knew that. I thought they liked to fight."

"No, it's just the other way round. When you hear men talk about how fine war is, and how they hope this country will have one some time soon, you can make up your mind that they are boasters and bullies, and that if a war really came they'd stay home and let someone else do the fighting. It isn't the people who talk the most and brag the loudest who step to the front when there's something really hard to be done. They leave that to the quiet people."

Then they walked along in silence. The place seemed even more beautiful now, but Bessie was too upset to appreciate its loveliness. She wondered if General Seeley would believe her, or if he would be more like Maw Hoover than Mrs. Chester.

"We'll find him on the porch in the back of the house, I think, Bessie. If he's there we can find him without going inside and bothering the servants. So we'll go around and see."

General Seeley was a small man, with white beard and moustache, and at her first look at him Bessie thought he looked very fierce indeed, and every inch a soldier, though there were so few inches. He had sharp blue eyes that were keen and piercing, and after he had risen and bowed to Mrs. Chester, which he did as soon as he saw her, he looked sharply at Bessie—so sharply that she was sure at once that he had judged her already, and was very angry at her.

"Well, well, so you've found the poacher and brought her with you, eh?" he said. "Sit down, ma'am, sit down, while I talk to her!"

And now Bessie saw that there was really a twinkle in the keen eyes, and that he wasn't as angry as he looked.

"What's her name? Bessie, eh? Bessie King? Well, sit down, Bessie, and we'll have a talk. No use standing up—none at all! Might as well be comfortable!"

"Thank you, sir," said Bessie, and sat down. She was still nervous, but her fright was lessened. He was much more kindly than she had expected him to be, somehow.

"Now, let's find out all about this, Bessie. Didn't you know you oughtn't to frighten the birds? Or didn't you think they'd be frightened—eh, what?"

Bessie didn't understand, fully, at first.

"But I didn't frighten them, sir," she said.

"They thought so. Stupid birds, eh, to think they were frightened when they weren't? But you remember they didn't know any better."

He laughed merrily at his own joke, and glanced at Mrs. Chester, as if he expected her to laugh, too, and to be amused, but her eyes were troubled, and she was very thoughtful.

"Come, come," he went on. "It's not so very terrible, after all! We've all of us done things we were sorry for—eh, Mrs. Chester? I'll wager that even you have—and I know very well that there are lots of things I can think of that I did just because I didn't think there was any harm in them."

"Some people wouldn't admit that, General Seeley, but it's very true," said Mrs. Chester. "I know it is in my case."

"Well, well, can't you talk, Bessie? Aren't you going to tell me you're sorry and that you won't do it again?"

"I'm sorry the birds were frightened," said Bessie, bravely. "But I can't say that I won't do it again—"

"What's that? What's that? Bless me, what's the use of saying you're sorry if you mean to do it the next time you get a chance?"

The general was flushed as he spoke, and his eyes held the same angry look they had worn at first. Mrs. Chester sighed and decided that it was time for her to speak.

"I don't think that was just what Bessie meant, General. I think you didn't understand her—"

"Well, well, perhaps not! What do you mean, Bessie?"

"I mean I can't promise not to do it again, sir, because I didn't do it at all, in the first place. Really, I didn't—"

"Oh, nonsense!" said the general, testily. "I'm ready to overlook it—don't you understand that? All I want you to do is to confess, and to say you're sorry. Nothing's going to happen to you!"

"I can't confess when I didn't do it," pleaded Bessie. "And if I had done it, I'd say so, whether anything was going to happen to me or not. That wouldn't make any difference."

General Seeley jumped to his feet.

"Oh, come, come! That's nonsense!" he said. "Who else could have done it, eh? Answer me that! I've said I'd forgive you—"

"But, General," protested Mrs. Chester, "if Bessie didn't do it, she'd be telling you an untruth if she said she had—and you wouldn't have her do that?"

"I'm a just man, Mrs. Chester, but I know what's what. She must have done it—she was around the place. And I know that none of my men did it. They know better! No one but the game-keepers are allowed to go into the preserve, and they all know they'd be dismissed at once if they disobeyed my rules about that. I'm strict—very strict! I insist upon obedience of orders and truthfulness—learned the need of them when I was in the army. Don't you think I can tell what's going on here, ma'am?"

"I think you're mistaken, General—that's all. I'm sure Bessie is telling the truth. Why shouldn't she? You've told her that she needn't be afraid to confess if she did frighten the birds, and that was very kind and generous of you. So, if she had, she wouldn't have anything to lose by saying so, and promising not to be careless that way again."

"What do you know about her, ma'am? Isn't it true that she's one of the two girls you told me about last night—that Miss Mercer had found? If—"

"I know she's a brave, honest girl, General. She's proved that already."

"I disagree with you, Mrs. Chester," said the general, stiffly. "You're a lady, and you naturally think well of everyone. I've learned by bitter experience that we can't always do that. I've trusted men, and had them go wrong, despite that. If she was one of the girls like the others, that you'd always known about, it would be different. Then I'd be happy to take your word for it. But when I think you aren't in any better position to judge than I am, I've got to use my own judgment."

"I'm sorry, General," said Mrs. Chester. "I can't tell you how sorry I am—but I'm sure you're wrong."

"She can't stay here, that's certain," said the general, testily. "I can't have a girl about the place who frightens my birds and then tells—lies—"

Bessie cried out sharply at that word.

"Oh—oh!" she said. "Really, I've told the truth—I have, indeed! If I said what you want me to say, than I'd be lying—but I'm not."

"Silence, please!" said General Seeley, sternly. "I'm talking with Mrs. Chester now, young woman. You've had your chance—and you wouldn't take it. Now I'm done with you!"

"What do you mean, General?" asked Mrs. Chester, looking very grave.

"You'll have to send her away—where she came from, Mrs. Chester. You and the girls you can vouch for are welcome, but I can't have her here."

"I can't do that, General," said Mrs. Chester, not angrily, but gravely, and looking him straight in the eyes.

"But you must! I won't let her stay here! And these are my grounds, aren't they?"

"Certainly! But if Bessie goes, we all go with her. It's not our way to desert those we've once befriended and taken in, General."

"That is for you to decide, ma'am," he said, stiffly. He got up and bowed to her. "I'm sorry that this should cause a quarrel—"

"It hasn't," said Mrs. Chester, smiling. "It takes two to make a quarrel, and I simply won't quarrel with you, General. I know you'll be sorry for what you've said when you think it over. Come, Bessie!"

Bessie, quite stunned by the trouble that had come upon them so suddenly out of a clear sky, couldn't speak for a minute.

"Oh," she said, then, "you don't mean that all the girls will have to leave this lovely place because of me?"

"Not because of you, but because of a mistake that's not your fault, Bessie. You mustn't worry about it. Just leave it to me. I'm sure you're telling the truth, and I'm going to stick by you."

CHAPTER XIV

THE TRUTH AT LAST

But Bessie, despite Mrs. Chester's kind words, was terribly downcast.

"Really, Mrs. Chester," she said miserably, "it's awfully unfair to make all the other girls suffer on account of me."

"You mustn't look at it that way, Bessie. You couldn't tell a lie, you know, even to prevent this trouble."

"No, but I'm sure he thinks I did that. He's not an unkind man, and he really doesn't want to make me unhappy, and drive you all away, I know. Mrs. Chester, won't you send me away?"

"Nonsense, Bessie! If you haven't done anything wrong, why shouldn't we stand by you? Even if you had, we'd do that, and we ought to do it all the more when you're in the right, and unjustly suspected. Don't you worry about it a bit! Everything will be all right."

"But I really think you ought to let me go. I'm just a trouble maker—I make trouble for everyone! If it hadn't been for me, Jake Hoover would never have burnt his father's barn—don't you know that?"

"That isn't so, Bessie. If you hadn't been there, something else would have happened. And it's the same way here. You haven't anything to do with all this trouble here. It would have come just the same if you hadn't arrived at all, I'm sure of that. And then one of the girls would have been accused, and everything would have happened just the same."

"Oh, I'm afraid not!"

"But I'm sure of it, Bessie, and I really know better than you. You mustn't take it so hard. No one is going to blame you. Rest easy about that. I'll see to it that they all understand just how it is."

"I wish I could believe that!"

Mrs. Chester told Eleanor what General Seeley had said as soon as they returned to the camp, and Eleanor, after a moment, just laughed.

"Well, it can't be helped," she said. "If he wants to act that way, we can't stop him, can we? And I'm so glad that you're going to stick by poor Bessie. I know she feels as bad as she can feel about it—and it's so fine for her to know that she really has some friends who will trust her and believe her at last. She's never had them before."

"She has them now, Eleanor. And it's because you're so fond of her already that I'm so sure she's telling the truth. I think I'd trust her, anyhow, but, even if I'd never seen her, I'd take your word."

"Will you tell all the girls why we're going?"

"I think not—just at first, anyhow. We'll just say that we're going to move on. I'm pretty sure that the people over at Pine Bridge will have some place where we can make camp, and that we can have our Council Fire to-night just the same. It won't be as nice as it is here, of course, but we'll make it do, somehow."

So Mrs. Chester went around to the different Guardians of the Camp Fires, and told them of the change in the plans. At once the order to strike the tents and pack was given, and then Mrs. Chester went to make arrangements for carrying the baggage over to Pine Bridge and for getting a camping place there.

"I'll get back as soon as I can, Eleanor," she said, "but I may be delayed in finding a camping place. If I am, I'll send the wagons over—I don't want to use General Seeley's, while he's angry at us. And you can take charge and see that everything goes as it should. You'll just take my place."

"No one can do that, Mrs. Chester, but I'll do my best."

Bessie, forlorn and unhappy, helped in the work of packing, and longed for someone to talk to. She didn't want to tell Zara, who had troubles enough of her own to worry her, and Eleanor, of course, was too busy, with all the work of seeing that everything was done properly. She had to keep a watchful eye on the preparations of the other Camp Fires as well as of her own. And then, suddenly, Bessie got a new idea.

"All this trouble is for me," she said. "Suppose I weren't here—suppose I just went away? Then they could all stay."

The more she thought of that, the more the idea grew upon her.

"I will do that—I will!" she said to herself, with sudden determination. "I'm just like a sign of bad luck—I make trouble for everyone who's good to me. Like Paw Hoover! He was always good—and the fire hurt him more than it did anyone else, though it was Maw Hoover and Jake who made all my trouble. I won't stay here and let them suffer for me any longer."

And, very quietly, since she wanted no one to know what she was doing, Bessie went into the tent, which had not yet been taken down, and changed from the blouse and skirt, which had been lent to her, into the old dress she had worn when she had jumped into the water to rescue Minnehaha.

Then, moving as silently and as cautiously as she could, Bessie slipped into the woods behind the camp. She dared not go the other way, which was the direct route to the main road outside of General Seeley's estate, because she knew that if any of the girls, or one of the Guardians saw her, she would be stopped. She didn't know the way by the direction she had to take, but she was sure that she could find it, and she wasn't afraid. Her one idea was to get away and save trouble for the others.

Of course, if Bessie had stopped to think, she would have known that it was wrong to do what she planned. But her aim was unselfish, and she didn't think of the grief and anxiety that would follow her disappearance. She was sensitive, in any case, and General Seeley's stern manner, although he had not really meant to be unkind, had upset her dreadfully.

To her surprise, the woods that she followed grew very thick. And she was still more surprised, presently, to come upon a wire fence. In such woods, it seemed very strange to her. Then, as she saw a bird with a long, brilliantly colored tail strutting around on the other side of the fence, she suddenly understood. This must be the place where the precious pheasants she was supposed to have frightened were kept. And she hadn't even known where they were!

Bessie wondered, as she looked at the beautiful bird, how anyone could have the heart to frighten it, or any like it.

"I don't blame General Seeley a bit for being angry if he really thought I had done that," she said to herself. "And he did, of course. They don't know anything about me, really. He was quite right."

Then she remembered, too, what he had said about the game-keepers. Probably, after what had happened, they would be more careful than ever, and Bessie decided that she had better move along as fast as she could, lest someone find her and think she was trying to get at the birds again.

But, anxious as she was to get away from the dangerous neighborhood, she found that, to move at all, she had to stick close to the fence, since the going beyond it was too rough for her. Then, too, as she went along, she heard strange noises—as if someone was moving in the woods near her, and trying not to make a noise. That frightened and puzzled her, so she moved very quietly herself, anxious to find out who it was. A wild thought came to her, too—perhaps it was the real poacher, for whom she had been mistaken, that she heard!

Presently the fence turned out, and she had to circle around, following it, to keep to the straight path. And, as the fence turned in again, she gave a sudden gasping little cry, that she had the greatest difficulty in choking down, lest it betray her at once.

For she saw a dark figure against the green background, bending over, and plucking at something that lay on the ground.

"It is! It really is—the poacher!" she whispered to herself.

She longed to know what to do. There was no way of telling whether there was anyone about. If she lifted her voice and called for help, it might bring a game-keeper quickly—and it might simply give the poacher the alarm, and enable him to escape, leaving the evidence of the crime to be turned against her. And this time no one, not even Mrs. Chester, would believe in her innocence.

Slowly Bessie crept toward the crouching figure. At least she would try to see his face, so that she would recognize him again, if she was lucky enough to see him. For Bessie was determined that some time, no matter how far in the future, she would clear herself, and make General Seeley admit that he had wronged her.

And then, when she was scarcely ten feet from him, she stepped on a branch that crackled under her feet, and the poacher turned and faced her, springing to his feet. Bessie screamed as she saw his face, for it was her old enemy—Jake Hoover!

For a moment he was far more frightened than she. He stared at her stupidly. Then he recognized her, and his face showed his evil triumph.

"Ah, here, are yer?" he cried, and sprang toward her, his hands full of the feathers he had plucked from the tail of the pheasant he had snared.

That move was Jake's fatal mistake. Had he run at once, he might have been able to escape. But now, Bessie, brave as ever, sprang to meet him. He was far stronger than she, but she had seen help approaching—a man in velveteens, and for just a moment after Jake, too, had seen the game-keeper, Bessie was able to keep him from running. She clung to his arms and legs, and though Jake struck at her, she would not let go. And then, just in time, the game-keeper's heavy hand fell on Jake's shoulder.

"So you're the poacher, my lad?" he said. "Well I've caught you this time, dead to rights."

Squirm and wriggle as he would, Jake couldn't escape now. He was trapped at last, and for once Bessie saw that he was going to reap the reward of his evil doing.

The game-keeper lifted a whistle to his lips, and blew a loud, long blast upon it. In a moment the wood filled with the noise of men approaching, and, to Bessie's delight, she saw General Seeley among them.

"What? At it again?" he said, angrily, as he saw Bessie. Jake was hidden by the game-keeper, and General Seeley thought at first that it was Bessie who had fallen to the trap he had set. Bessie said nothing—she couldn't.

"No, General. It wasn't the girl, after all," said the game-keeper. "Never did seem to me as if it could be, anyhow. Here's the lad that did it all—and I caught him in the act. The feathers are all over him still."

"It wasn't me! She did it! I saw her, and I took the feathers from her," wailed Jake, anxious, as ever, to escape himself, no matter how many lies he had to tell, or who had to suffer for his sins. But the game-keeper only laughed roughly.

"That won't do you no good, my boy. You'd better own up and take your medicine. Here, see this, General."

He plunged his hands into Jake's pockets, and produced the wire and other materials Jake had used in making his snare.

"I guess that's pretty good evidence, ain't it, sir?"

"It is, indeed," said the general, grimly. "Take him up to the house, Tyler. I'll attend to his case later. Go on, now. I want to talk to this girl."

Then he turned to Bessie and took off his hat.

"I was wrong and you were right this morning," he said, pleasantly. "I want to apologize to you, Bessie. And I shall try to make up to you for having treated you so badly. How can I do that?"

"Oh, there's nothing to make up, General," said Bessie, tearfully. "I'm so glad you know I didn't do that!"

"But what are you doing here—and in that dress?"

"I—I was going away—so that the others could stay."

"I see—so that they wouldn't have to suffer because I was so brutally unkind to you. Well, you come with me! Why didn't you wear the other clothes, though? They're nicer than these."

"They're not mine. These are all I have, of my own."

"Is that so? Well, you shall have the best wardrobe money can buy, Bessie, just as soon as Mrs. Chester can get it for you. I'll make that my present to you—as a way of making up, partly, for the way I behaved to you. How will you like that?"

"That's awfully good of you, but you mustn't—really, you mustn't!"

"I guess I can do as I like with my own money, Bessie. And I'm going to be one of your friends—one of your best friends, if you'll let me. Will you shake hands, to show that you don't bear any hard feelings?"

And Bessie, unable to speak, held out her hand.

General Seeley wrung it—then he started, suddenly.

"Here, here, what am I thinking of?" he said, briskly. "I must find Mrs. Chester and ask her to forgive me. Do you think she will do it, Bessie? Or haven't you known her long enough—"

"Why should she forgive you, sir? You just thought what anyone else would have thought. What I don't understand is why she was willing to believe me. She didn't know anything about me—"

"I'll tell you why, Bessie. It's because she knows human nature, and I, like the old fool I am, wouldn't acknowledge it! But I've learned my lesson—I'll never venture to disagree with her again. And I'm going to hunt her up and tell her so."

So Bessie, as happy as she had been miserable a few minutes before, went with the general, while he looked for Mrs. Chester. She returned from Pine Bridge just as they reached the camp, and she listened to General Seeley's apologies with smiling eyes.

"I knew I was right," was all she said. "And I'm more than glad that the real culprit was found. But, my dear, you oughtn't to have tried to leave us that way. It wasn't your fault, and we should have gone, just the same, and we would have had to look for you until we found you. When we once make friends of anyone, we don't let them get away from us. That wouldn't be true to the spirit of the Camp Fire—not a bit of it!"

Then, while Bessie changed again into the clothes Ayu had lent her, Mrs. Chester gave the welcome order to unpack, and explained to the Guardians that Bessie was cleared, and they were going to stay in camp, and have the Council Fire just as it had been planned. Everyone was delighted, Eleanor Mercer most of all, because she had had real faith in Bessie, and it was a triumph for her to know that her faith had not been misplaced.

CHAPTER XV

THE COUNCIL FIRE

The girls of the Manasquan Camp Fire did little that day except to cook their meals and keep the camp in order. The order to unpack had come, fortunately, in time to save a lot of trouble, since very little had been done toward preparing to move, and, when it was all over, Eleanor called the girls together, and told them just what had happened.

"There is a fine lesson for all of us in that," she said. "If Bessie had been weak, she might very well have been tempted to say what General Seeley wanted her to say. She knew she hadn't done anything wrong—and she said so. But she was told that if she would confess she wouldn't be punished, or even scolded, and still she would not do it, even when she found that it meant trouble for her and for us. And, you see, she earned the reward of doing the right thing, for the truth came out. And it will happen that way most of the time—ninety-nine times out of a hundred, I believe."

"I should think you'd be perfectly furious at Jake Hoover, Bessie," said Zara. "He makes trouble for you all the time. Here he got you blamed for something he'd done again, and nearly spoiled things just when they were beginning to look better."

"But he didn't know that, Zara. He did something wrong, but he couldn't have known that I was going to be blamed for it, you know."

"Aren't you angry at him at all?"

"Yes, for killing that beautiful bird with his horrid snare. But I'm sorry for him, too. I think he didn't know any better."

"What will happen to him, do you think, Bessie! Will he be sent to prison?"

"I don't believe so. General Seeley is a kind man, and I think he'll try to make Jake understand how wrong it was to act so, and send him home. I certainly hope so."

"I don't see why. I should think you'd want him to be punished. He's done so many mean things without being found out that when he is caught, he ought to get what he deserves."

"But it wouldn't be punishing just him, you see, Zara. It would be hard for Paw Hoover, too, and you know how good he was to us. If it hadn't been for him I don't believe we'd ever have got to Pine Bridge at all."

"Yes, that's so. He was good to us, Bessie. I'd like to see him again, and tell him so. But I can't—not if Farmer Weeks can get me if I ever go back into that state."

"There's another thing to think of, too, Zara, about Jake. He's more likely to be found out now, when he does something wrong."

"Oh, yes, that's true, isn't it? I hadn't thought of that. He won't be able to make Maw Hoover think you did everything now, when you're not there, will he?"

"That's just what I mean. And maybe, when she finds that the things she used to blame me for keep on happening just the same, though I'm not there, she'll see that I never did do them at all. It looked pretty bad for me this morning, Zara, but you see it came out all right. And I'm beginning to think now that other things will turn out right, too, just as Miss Eleanor's been saying they would."

"Oh, I do hope so! There's Miss Eleanor coming now."

"Well, girls, have you chosen your fire names yet?" asked the Guardian. "You'll have to be ready to tell us to-night at the big fire you know, when you get your rings."

"Why, I hadn't thought about it, even. Had you, Zara?"

"Yes, I had. I think I'd like to be called by a name that would make people think of being happy and cheerful. Is there an Indian word that would do that?"

"Perhaps. But why don't you make up a new word for yourself, as we made up Wo-he-lo? You could take the first letters of happy and cheerful, and call yourself Hachee. That sounds like an Indian word, though it really isn't. And what for a symbol?"

"I think a chipmunk is the happiest, cheerfulest thing I know."

"That's splendid! You can be Hachee, and your symbol shall be the chipmunk. You've done well, Zara. I don't think you'll ever want to burn your name."

"What is that? Burning one's name?" inquired Zara.

"Sometimes a girl chooses a name and later she doesn't like it. Then, at a Council Fire, she writes that name, the one she wants to give up, on a slip of paper, and it's thrown into the fire. And after that she is never called by it again."

"Oh, I see. No, I like my new name and I'll want to keep that, I know."

"I've always liked the name of Stella—that means a star, doesn't it?—so that my name and my symbol could be the same, if I took that."

"Yes, Bessie. That's a good choice, too. You shall be Stella, when we are using the ceremonial names. Well, that's settled, then. You must learn to repeat the Wood-Gatherer's desire to-night—and after that you will get your rings, and then you will be real Camp Fire Girls, like the rest of us."

Then she left them, because there was much for her to do, and that afternoon Bessie and Zara made very sure that they knew the Wood-Gatherer's desire, and learned all that the other girls could tell them about the law of the fire, and all the other things they wanted to know. But they waited anxiously for it to be time to light the great Council Fire.

All afternoon the Wood-Gatherers worked, gathering the fagots for the fire, and arranging them neatly. They were built up so that there was a good space for a draught under the wood, in order that the fire, once it was lighted, might burn clear and bright. A cloudless summer sky gave promise of a beautiful starlit night, so that there was no danger of a repetition of the disappointment of the previous night—which, however, everyone had already forgotten.

After supper, when it was quite dark, the space around the pile was left empty. Then Mrs. Chester, in her ceremonial Indian robes, stood up in the centre, near the fire, and one by one the different Camp Fires, led by their Guardians, came in, singing slowly.

As each girl passed before her, Mrs. Chester made the sign of the Fire, by raising her right hand slowly, in a sweeping gesture, after first crossing its fingers against those of the left hand. Each girl returned the sign and then passed to her place in the great circle about the fagots, where she sat down.

When all the girls were seated, Mrs. Chester spoke.

"The Manasquan Camp Fire has the honor of lighting our Council Fire to-night," she said. "Ayu!"

And Ayu stepped forward. She had with her the simple tools that are required for making fire in the Indian fashion. It is not enough, as some people believe, to rub two sticks together, and Bessie and Zara, who had never seen this trick played before, watched her with great interest. Ayu had, first, a block of wood, not very thick, in which a notch had been cut. In this notch she rested a long, thin stick, and on top of that was a small piece of wood, in which the stick or drill rested. And, last of all, she had a bow, with a leather thong, which was slipped around the drill.

When everything was ready Ayu, holding down the fire block with one foot, held the socket of the drill with the left hand, while with the right she drew the bow rapidly back and forth. In less than a minute there was a tiny spark. Then rapidly growing, flame appeared and a moment later, along the carefully prepared tinder, the fire ran to the kindling beneath the fagots. And then, as the flames rose and began to curl about the fagots all the girls began to sing together the Camp Fire Girl Ode to Fire:

"Oh Fire!

Long years ago when our fathers fought with great animals you were their protection.

From the cruel cold of winter you saved them.

When they needed food you changed the flesh of beasts into savory food for them.

During all the ages your mysterious flame has been a symbol to them for Spirit.

So to-night we light our fire in remembrance of the Great Spirit who gave you to us."

Then each Guardian called the roll of her Camp Fire, and as each girl's ceremonial name was called she answered, "Kolah!"

"That means friend," someone whispered to Bessie and Zara.

"We are to receive two new members to-night," said Mrs. Chester, then. "Wanaka, they come in your Camp Fire. Will you initiate them into the Camp Fire circle?"

Then she sat down, and Wanaka took her place in the centre. Bessie and Zara understood that it was time for them to step forward, and they stood out in the dancing light of the fire, which was roaring up now, and casting its light into the shadows about the circle. All the girls stood up.

Bessie came first, and Wanaka turned to her.

"Is it your desire to become a Camp Fire Girl and follow the law of the Fire?"

And Bessie, who had been taught the form to be followed, answered:

"It is my desire to become a Camp Fire Girl and to obey the law of the Camp Fire, which is to Seek Beauty, Give Service, Pursue Knowledge, Be Trustworthy, Hold on to Health, Glorify Work, Be Happy. This law of the Camp Fire I will strive to follow."

Then she held out her left hand, and Eleanor took it, saying:

"In the name of the Camp Fire Girls of America, I place on the little finger of your left hand this ring, with its design of seven fagots, symbolic of the seven points of the law of the Fire, which you have expressed your desire to follow, and of the three circles on either side, symbolic of the three watchwords of this organization—Work, Health, and Love. And—

"As fagots are brought from the forest

Firmly held by the sinews which bind them,

So cleave to these others, your sisters,

Whoever, whenever, you find them.

"Be strong as the fagots are sturdy;

Be pure in your deepest desire;

Be true to the truth that is in you;

And—follow the law of the Fire."

Then, as Bessie, or Stella, as, at the Council Fire she was to be known thereafter, made her way back to her place, all the girls sang the Wo-he-lo song by way of welcoming her as one of them.

Then it was Zara's turn, and the same beautiful ceremony was repeated for her.

"Now the Snug Harbor Camp Fire is going to entertain us with some new Indian dances they have learned," said Mrs. Chester. "I am sure we will all enjoy that."

And they did. No Indian girls ever danced with the grace and beauty that those young American girls put into their interpretation of the old-fashioned dances, which made all the other Camp Fires determine to try to learn them, too. And after that there was a talk from Mrs. Chester on the purpose of the organization. Then, finally, taps sounded, and the Council Fire was over.

"So you really are Camp Fire Girls," said Eleanor, to the two new members. "Soon we shall be back in the city and there I am sure that many things will happen to you. Some of them will be hard, but you will get through them all right. And remember we mean to help you, no matter what happens. Zara shall have her father back, and we will do all we can, Bessie, to help you find your parents. Good-night!"

"Good-night!"